WHAT THEY'VE SAID ABOUT LAWRENCE BLOCK AND MATTHEW SCUDDER

"When Lawrence Block is in his Matt Scudder mode, crime fiction can sidle up so close to literature that often there's no degree of difference."

~*Philadelphia Inquirer*

"One of the very best writers now working the beat. Block has done something new and remarkable with the private-eye novel."

~*Wall Street Journal*

"Block's prose is as smooth as aged whiskey."

~*Publishers Weekly*

"One of the most complex and compelling heroes in modern fiction. Thrillers don't get better than this."

~*San Diego Union-Tribune*

"After twenty-five years in the business, Matt Scudder still strolls New York's mean streets as if he had personally laid the cobblestones."

~*Marilyn Stasio, New York Times Book Review*

"Matthew Scudder is the kind of mystery anti-hero who turns mere readers into series addicts."

~*Atlanta Journal-Constitution*

THE NIGHT
AND THE MUSIC

The Matthew Scudder Stories

LAWRENCE BLOCK

TELEMACHUS
PRESS

This book is a work of fiction. Names, characters, places and incidents are either the product of the author's imagination or are used fictitiously. Any resemblance to actual persons, living or dead, or to actual events or locales is entirely coincidental.

The Night and The Music - *The Matthew Scudder Stories*

The publisher does not have any control over and does not assume any responsibility for author or third-party websites or their content.

Cover by: Telemachus Press, LLC
Copyright © BIGSTOCK/1271515

Visit the author's websites:
http://www.lawrenceblock.com
http://lawrenceblock.wordpress.com

Published by Telemachus Press, LLC
http://www.TelemachusPress.com

ISBN: 978-1-937387-31-0 (eBook)
ISBN: 978-1-937698-07-2 (EPUB)
ISBN: 978-1-937387-32-7 (Paperback)
ISBN: 978-1-937698-21-8 (Limited Edition)

Printed in the United States of America

10 9 8 7 6 5 4 3 2 1

FOR DANNY BAROR

TABLE OF CONTENTS

GROWING UP WITH MATTHEW SCUDDER

an appreciation by Brian Koppelman

Right around the time I turned fourteen, in 1980, I convinced my parents to let me take the Long Island Rail Road into Manhattan by myself, so I could go to the Mysterious Bookshop on West 56th Street. And it was there, in Otto Penzler's place between Sixth and Seventh avenues, that I first met Matt Scudder.

Mysterious was an intimidating place, especially for a bookshop. There was a step down entrance, and a heavy door that swung shut behind you. Once inside, it was dead quiet: no elevator music playing. No friendly info desk. No other customers either. Just a silent bearded guy behind the front counter who had an uncanny (and slightly disturbing) resemblance to Stephen King's 1970s author photo. I'm telling you, for a place designed to sell books, it was pretty damned intense.

I was mostly reading spy books back then. But on the day I took my maiden solo voyage on the LIRR Port Washington line, I was looking for something else. I just didn't know what, exactly. Which was a bummer because that meant I was going to have to talk to spooky

1

Stephen King behind the counter, and he was reading and seemed very involved in his book and not at all in the mood to be disturbed by some teenager from Nassau County.

So I just kind of stood around aimlessly until his eyes hovered for a moment above his book. And then I gutted up and asked him for a recommendation.

"What do you like?" he asked.

I mumbled something along the lines of "A bunch of stuff. "

"You into funny books?"

"Not really," I said, "I guess I like when it feels like it's really happening."

"Oh," he said, "You might be ready for something hard boiled."

Hard Boiled. I had never heard the phrase before. But it sounded just right. Especially if it was something I had to "be ready" for.

"Yes," I said, "give me something hard boiled."

And he reached up behind the counter and grabbed three books.

"This is what you need," he said. And he held out the books—*The Sins Of The Fathers, Time To Murder and Create* and *In The Midst Of Death*. "They're by Lawrence Block."

I paid for them, headed back to Penn Station, caught the next train, found a seat and started reading *Sins* before the train had even begun to roll.

Fifty-five minutes later, I almost missed my stop.

My mom picked me up from the station, but I don't think I said two words to her on the drive home; I just kept reading. And I remember walking in our front door, nodding to my sisters and continuing on to my bedroom reading the entire way.

Fake Stephen King had gotten it right. Matt Scudder was, indeed, exactly what I needed.

I blasted through all three books. I'm not sure how I was able to lock into Scudder so hard when our life experience was so far apart--I had never had a drink, had never killed anyone, either on purpose or by accident, had barely kissed a girl--but somehow he made sense to me.

Maybe it's because there was nothing phony about Matt Scudder. When Matt wanted to drink, he drank. When he wanted to fight, he fought. And if he didn't want to talk to you, he didn't. Hell, even if you were his client, he wouldn't try and charm you, wouldn't promise to solve your case, wouldn't even promise to tell you what he was doing to try and solve it.

Scudder was no innocent. He knew the world was essentially crooked. But that didn't mean he had to bend to it. He might pay off a cop for information, but he wouldn't lie to himself about what it meant, and the ultimate price he might have to pay for doing so.

To a teenager like me, just beginning to learn all the ways in which the world presses you to compromise the best of yourself, just starting to figure out that most grown-ups were liars, Matt Scudder's refusal to play along with anyone else's bullshit spoke directly to me. And Scudder was such a flawed, broken hero. All the spies I had been reading about were almost superhuman. Scudder was barely hanging on to whatever was left of his humanity, his skills, his character. He knew it. Told the reader about it. And I loved him for it.

I still love him for it. Some time after finishing *In The Midst Of Death,* I resolved to read every book ever written about Scudder. Unlike almost every other promise I made to myself in my teens, this one I've kept. Luckily for me, the books have only gotten better. At some point, consciously or not, Larry Block made a decision to fuse big giant chunks of himself with his character. And so Matt Scudder has aged, has quit drinking, has quit whoring, has quit...has quit almost everything, only to be lured back in again when something makes him angry or invested enough to care. And so I continue to care, even as my visits to the (now downtown) Mysterious Bookshop have become far less frequent, even as my time spent reading fiction has become far less frequent, even as my fourteen-year old self seems further and further away from who I am now.

I have a fifteen year old son. And two weeks back he took his first solo train voyage. This one to Washington DC. He needed a book for the journey. So I walked him over to the bookshelf, pulled down *The Sins Of The Fathers* and told him, "This is what you need." He smiled. But not half as much as I did.

The last story in this collection is about Matt and Mick Ballou. Over the past twenty years, their friendship has become the soul of the series and means more to me than any other friendship in fiction. It is the one nod to the romantic that Lawrence Block is willing to give us in the Matt Scudder books. The one nod to possibility, to hope, to brotherhood, acceptance, honor and truth between people. But mostly, there is forgiveness. The very act of those two men sitting across from one another late into the night is forgiveness. The talking, sometimes laughing, sometimes just sitting quietly until the morning light starts leaking in through Grogan's windows, means that there is a safe harbor for each of us, where no one sits in judgment, where no one condemns, where we can be exactly who we are, ruined, sinful, wracked. They are flawed, Matt and Mick, but they are perfect. And when we spend time with them, we believe we are too.

THE NIGHT AND THE MUSIC

The Matthew Scudder Stories

OUT THE WINDOW

There was nothing special about her last day. She seemed a little jittery, preoccupied with something or with nothing at all. But this was nothing new for Paula.

She was never much of a waitress in the three months she spent at Armstrong's. She'd forget some orders and mix up others, and when you wanted the check or another round of drinks you could go crazy trying to attract her attention. There were days when she walked through her shift like a ghost through walls, and it was as though she had perfected some arcane technique of astral projection, sending her mind out for a walk while her long lean body went on serving food and drinks and wiping down empty tables.

She did make an effort, though. She damn well tried. She could always manage a smile. Sometimes it was the brave smile of the walking wounded and other times it was a tight-jawed, brittle grin with a couple tabs of amphetamine behind it, but you take what you can to get through the days and any smile is better than none at all. She knew most of Armstrong's regulars by name

7

and her greeting always made you feel as though you'd come home. When that's all the home you have, you tend to appreciate that sort of thing.

And if the career wasn't perfect for her, well, it certainly hadn't been what she'd had in mind when she came to New York in the first place. You no more set out to be a waitress in a Ninth Avenue gin mill than you intentionally become an ex-cop coasting through the months on bourbon and coffee. We have that sort of greatness thrust upon us. When you're as young as Paula Wittlauer you hang in there, knowing things are going to get better. When you're my age you just hope they don't get too much worse.

She worked the early shift, noon to eight, Tuesday through Saturday. Trina came on at six so there were two girls on the floor during the dinner rush. At eight Paula would go wherever she went and Trina would keep on bringing cups of coffee and glasses of bourbon for another six hours or so.

Paula's last day was a Thursday in late September. The heat of the summer was starting to break up. There was a cooling rain that morning and the sun never did show its face. I wandered in around four in the afternoon with a copy of the *Post* and read through it while I had my first drink of the day. At eight o'clock I was talking with a couple of nurses from Roosevelt Hospital who wanted to grouse about a resident surgeon with a Messiah complex. I was making sympathetic noises when Paula swept past our table and told me to have a good evening.

I said, "You too, kid." Did I look up? Did we smile at each other? Hell, I don't remember.

"See you tomorrow, Matt."

"Right," I said. "God willing."

But He evidently wasn't. Around three Justin closed up and I went around the block to my hotel. It didn't take long for the coffee and bourbon to cancel each other out. I got into bed and slept.

My hotel is on Fifty-seventh Street between Eighth and Ninth. It's on the uptown side of the block and my window is on the street side looking south. I can see the World Trade Center at the tip of Manhattan from my window.

I can also see Paula's building. It's on the other side of Fifty-seventh Street a hundred yards or so to the east, a towering high-rise that, had it been directly across from me, would have blocked my view of the trade center.

She lived on the seventeenth floor. Sometime after four she went out a high window. She swung out past the sidewalk and landed in the street a few feet from the curb, touching down between a couple of parked cars.

In high school physics they teach you that falling bodies accelerate at a speed of thirty-two feet per second. So she would have fallen thirty-two feet in the first second, another sixty-four feet the next second, then ninety-six feet in the third. Since she fell something like two hundred feet, I don't suppose she could have spent more than four seconds in the actual act of falling.

It must have seemed a lot longer than that.

I got up around ten, ten-thirty. When I stopped at the desk for my mail Vinnie told me they'd had a jumper across the street during the night. "A dame," he said, which is a word you don't hear much anymore. "She went out without a stitch on. You could catch your death that way."

I looked at him.

"Landed in the street, just missed somebody's Caddy. How'd you like to find something like that for a hood ornament? I wonder if your insurance would cover that. What do you call it, act of God?" He came out from behind the desk and walked with me to the door. "Over there," he said, pointing. "The florist's van there is covering the spot where she flopped. Nothing to see anyway. They scooped her up with a spatula and a sponge and then they hosed it all down. By the time I came on duty there wasn't a trace left."

"Who was she?"

"Who knows?"

I had things to do that morning, and as I did them I thought from time to time of the jumper. They're not that rare and they usually do the deed in the hours before dawn. They say it's always darkest then.

Sometime in the early afternoon I was passing Armstrong's and stopped in for a short one. I stood at the bar and looked around to say hello to Paula but she wasn't there. A doughy redhead named Rita was taking her shift.

Dean was behind the bar. I asked him where Paula was. "She skipping school today?"

"You didn't hear?"

"Jimmy fired her?"

He shook his head, and before I could venture any further guesses he told me.

I drank my drink. I had an appointment to see somebody about something, but suddenly it ceased to seem important. I put a dime in the phone and canceled my appointment and came back and had another drink. My hand was trembling slightly when I picked up the glass. It was a little steadier when I set it down.

I crossed Ninth Avenue and sat in St. Paul's for a while. Ten, twenty minutes. Something like that. I lit a candle for Paula and a few other candles for a few other corpses, and I sat there and thought about life and death and high windows. Around the time I left the police force I discovered that churches were very good places for thinking about that sort of thing.

After a while I walked over to her building and stood on the pavement in front of it. The florist's truck had moved on and I examined the street where she'd landed. There was, as Vinnie had assured me, no trace of what had happened. I tilted my head back and looked up, wondering what window she might have fallen from, and then I looked down at the pavement and then up again, and a sudden rush of vertigo made my head spin. In the course of all this I managed to attract the attention of the building's doorman and he came out to the curb anxious to talk about the former tenant. He was a black man about my age and he looked as proud of his uniform as the guy in the Marine Corps recruiting poster. It was a good-looking uniform, shades of brown, epaulets, gleaming brass buttons.

"Terrible thing," he said. "A young girl like that with her whole life ahead of her."

"Did you know her well?"

He shook his head. "She would give me a smile, always say hello, always call me by name. Always in a hurry, rushing in, rushing out again. You wouldn't think she had a care in the world. But you never know."

"You never do."

"She lived on the seventeenth floor. I wouldn't live that high above the ground if you gave me the place rent-free."

"Heights bother you?"

I don't know if he heard the question. "I live up one flight of stairs. That's just fine for me. No elevator and no, no high window." His brow clouded and he looked on the verge of saying something else, but then someone started to enter his building's lobby and he moved to intercept him. I looked up again, trying to count windows to the seventeenth floor, but the vertigo returned and I gave it up.

"Are you Matthew Scudder?"

I looked up. The girl who'd asked the question was very young, with long straight brown hair and enormous light brown eyes. Her face was open and defenseless and her lower lip was quivering. I said I was Matthew Scudder and pointed at the chair opposite mine. She remained on her feet.

"I'm Ruth Wittlauer," she said.

The name didn't register until she said, "Paula's sister." Then I nodded and studied her face for signs of a family resemblance. If they were there I couldn't find them. It was ten in the evening and Paula Wittlauer had been dead for eighteen hours and her sister was standing expectantly before me, her face a curious blend of determination and uncertainty.

I said, "I'm sorry. Won't you sit down? And will you have something to drink?"

"I don't drink."

"Coffee?"

"I've been drinking coffee all day. I'm shaky from all the damn coffee. Do I *have* to order something?"

She was on the edge, all right. I said, "No, of course not. You don't have to order anything." And I caught Trina's eye and warned her off and she nodded shortly and let us alone. I sipped my own coffee and watched Ruth Wittlauer over the brim of the cup.

"You knew my sister, Mr. Scudder."

"In a superficial way, as a customer knows a waitress."

"The police say she killed herself."

"And you don't think so?"

"I know she didn't."

I watched her eyes while she spoke and I was willing to believe she meant what she said. She didn't believe that Paula went out the window of her own accord, not for a moment. Of course, that didn't mean she was right.

"What do you think happened?"

"She was murdered." She made the statement quite matter-of-factly. "I know she was murdered. I think I know who did it."

"Who?"

"Cary McCloud."

"I don't know him."

"But it may have been somebody else," she went on. She lit a cigarette, smoked for a few moments in silence. "I'm pretty sure it was Cary," she said.

"Why?"

"They were living together." She frowned, as if in recognition of the fact that cohabitation was small evidence of murder. "He could do it," she said carefully. "That's why I think he did. I don't think just anyone could commit murder. In the heat of the moment, sure, I guess people fly off the handle, but to do it deliberately and throw someone out of a, out of a, to just deliberately throw someone out of a — "

I put my hand on top of hers. She had long small-boned hands and her skin was cool and dry to the touch. I thought she was going to cry or break or something but she didn't. It was just not going to be possible for her to say the word *window* and she would stall every time she came to it.

"What do the police say?"

"Suicide. They say she killed herself." She drew on the cigarette. "But they don't know her, they never knew her. If Paula wanted to kill herself she would have taken pills. She liked pills."

"I figured she took ups."

"Ups, tranquilizers, ludes, barbiturates. And she liked grass and she liked to drink." She lowered her eyes. My hand was still on top of hers and she looked at our two hands and I removed mine. "I don't do any of those things. I drink coffee, that's my one vice, and I don't even do that much because it makes me jittery. It's the coffee that's making me nervous tonight. Not...all of this."

"Okay."

"She was twenty-four. I'm twenty. Baby sister, square baby sister, except that was always how she *wanted* me to be. She did all these things and at the same time she told me not to do them, that it was a bad scene. I think she kept me straight. I really do. Not so much because of what she was saying as that I looked at the way she was living and what it was doing to her and I didn't want that for myself. I thought it was crazy, what she was doing to herself, but at the same time I guess I worshiped her, she was always my heroine. I loved her, God, I really did, I'm just starting to realize how much, and she's dead and he killed her, I *know* he killed her, I just know it."

After a while I asked her what she wanted me to do.

"You're a detective."

"Not in an official sense. I used to be a cop."

"Could you...find out what happened?"

"I don't know."

"I tried talking to the police. It was like talking to the wall. I can't just turn around and do nothing. Do you understand me?"

"I think so. Suppose I look into it and it still looks like suicide?"

"She didn't kill herself."

"Well, suppose I wind up thinking that she did."

She thought it over. "I still wouldn't have to believe it."

"No," I agreed. "We get to choose what we believe."

"I have some money." She put her purse on the table. "I'm the straight sister, I have an office job, I save money. I have five hundred dollars with me."

"That's too much to carry in this neighborhood."

"Is it enough to hire you?"

I didn't want to take her money. She had five hundred dollars and a dead sister, and parting with one wouldn't bring the other back to life. I'd have worked for nothing but that wouldn't have been good because neither of us would have taken it seriously enough.

And I have rent to pay and two sons to support, and Armstrong's charges for the coffee and the bourbon. I took four fifty-dollar bills from her and told her I'd do my best to earn them.

After Paula Wittlauer hit the pavement, a black-and-white from the Eighteenth Precinct caught the squeal and took charge of the case. One of the cops in the car was a guy named Guzik. I hadn't known him when I was on the force but we'd met since then. I didn't like him and I don't think he cared for me either, but he was reasonably honest and had struck me as competent. I got him on the phone the next morning and offered to buy him a lunch.

We met at an Italian place on Fifty-sixth Street. He had veal and peppers and a couple glasses of red wine. I wasn't hungry but I made myself eat a small steak.

Between bites of veal he said, "The kid sister, huh? I talked to her, you know. She's so clean and so pretty it could break your heart if you let it. And of course she don't want to believe sis did the Dutch act. I asked is she Catholic because then there's the religious angle but that wasn't it. Anyway your average priest'll stretch a point.

They're the best lawyers going, the hell, two thousand years of practice, they oughta be good. I took that attitude myself. I said, 'Look, there's all these pills. Let's say your sister had herself some pills and drank a little wine and smoked a little pot and then she went to the window for some fresh air. So she got a little dizzy and maybe she blacked out and most likely she never knew what was happening.' Because there's no question of insurance, Matt, so if she wants to think it's an accident I'm not gonna shout suicide in her ear. But that's what it says in the file."

"You close it out?"

"Sure. No question."

"She thinks murder."

He nodded. "Tell me something I don't know. She says this McCloud killed sis. McCloud's the boyfriend. Thing is he was at an after-hours club at Fifty-third and Twelfth about the time sis was going skydiving."

"You confirm that?"

He shrugged. "It ain't airtight. He was in and out of the place, he coulda doubled back and all, but there was the whole business with the door."

"What business?"

"She didn't tell you? Paula Wittlauer's apartment was locked and the chain bolt was on. The super unlocked the door for us but we had to send him back to the basement for a bolt cutter so's we could get through the chain bolt. You can only fasten the chain bolt from inside and you can only open the door a few inches with it on, so either Wittlauer launched her own self out the window or she was shoved out by Plastic Man, and then he went and slithered out the door without unhooking the chain bolt."

"Or the killer never left the apartment."

"Huh?"

"Did you search the apartment after the super came back and cut the chain for you?"

"We looked around, of course. There was an open window, there was a pile of clothes next to it. You know she went out naked, don't you?"

"Uh-huh."

"There was no burly killer crouching in the shrubbery, if that's what you're getting at."

"You checked the place carefully?"

"We did our job."

"Uh-huh. Look under the bed?"

"It was a platform bed. No crawl space under it."

"Closets?"

He drank some wine, put the glass down hard, glared at me. "What the hell are you getting at? You got reason to believe there was somebody in the apartment when we went in there?"

"Just exploring the possibilities."

"Jesus. You honestly think somebody's gonna be stupid enough to stay in the apartment after shoving her out of it? She musta been on the street ten minutes before we hit the building. If somebody did kill her, which never happened, but if they did they coulda been halfway to Texas by the time we hit the door, and don't that make more sense than jumping in the closet and hiding behind the coats?"

"Unless the killer didn't want to pass the doorman."

"So he's still got the whole building to hide in. Just the one man on the front door is the only security the building's got, anyway, and what does he amount to? And suppose he hides in the apartment and we happen to spot him. Then where is he? With his neck in the noose, that's where he is."

"Except you didn't spot him."

"Because he wasn't there, and when I start seeing

little men who aren't there is when I put in my papers and quit the department."

There was an unvoiced challenge in his words. I had quit the department, but not because I'd seen little men. One night some years ago I broke up a bar holdup and went into the street after the pair who'd killed the bartender. One of my shots went wide and a little girl died, and after that I didn't see little men or hear voices, not exactly, but I did leave my wife and kids and quit the force and start drinking on a more serious level. But maybe it all would have happened just that way even if I'd never killed Estrellita Rivera. People go through changes and life does the damnedest things to us all.

"It was just a thought," I said. "The sister thinks it's murder so I was looking for a way for her to be right."

"Forget it."

"I suppose. I wonder why she did it."

"Do they even need a reason? I went in the bathroom and she had a medicine cabinet like a drugstore. Ups, downs, sideways. Maybe she was so stoned she thought she could fly. That would explain her being naked. You don't fly with your clothes on. Everybody knows that."

I nodded. "They find drugs in her system?"

"Drugs in her...oh, Jesus, Matt. She came down seventeen flights and she came down fast."

"Under four seconds."

"Huh?"

"Nothing," I said. I didn't bother telling him about high school physics and falling bodies. "No autopsy?"

"Of course not. You've seen jumpers. You were in the department a lot of years, you know what a person looks like after a drop like that. You want to be technical, there coulda been a bullet in her and nobody was gonna go and look for it. Cause of death was falling from a great height. That's what it says and that's what it was, and don't ask me was she stoned or was she pregnant or any of those questions because who the hell knows and who the hell cares, right?"

"How'd you even know it was her?"

"We got a positive ID from the sister."

I shook my head. "I mean how did you know what apartment to go to? She was naked so she didn't have any identification on her. Did the doorman recognize her?"

"You kidding? He wouldn't go close enough to look. He was alongside the building throwing up a few pints of cheap wine. He couldn't have identified his own ass."

"Then how'd you know who she was?"

"The window." I looked at him. "Hers was the only window that was open more than a couple of inches, Matt. Plus her lights were on. That made it easy."

"I didn't think of that."

"Yeah, well, I was there, and we just looked up and there was an open window and a light behind it, and that was the first place we went to. You'da thought of it if you were there."

"I suppose."

He finished his wine, burped delicately against the back of his hand. "It's suicide," he said. "You can tell the sister as much."

"I will. Okay if I look at the apartment?"

"Wittlauer's apartment? We didn't seal it, if that's what you mean. You oughta be able to con the super out of a key."

"Ruth Wittlauer gave me a key."

"Then there you go. There's no department seal on the door. You want to look around?"

"So I can tell the sister I was there."

"Yeah. Maybe you'll come across a suicide note. That's what I was looking for, a note. You turn up something like that and it clears up doubts for the friends and relatives. If it was up to me I'd get a law passed. No suicide without a note."

"Be hard to enforce."

"Simple," he said. "If you don't leave a note you gotta come back and be alive again." He laughed. "That'd start 'em scribbling away. Count on it."

The doorman was the same man I'd talked to the day before. It never occurred to him to ask me my business. I rode up in the elevator and walked along the corridor to 17G. The key Ruth Wittlauer had given me opened the door. There was just the one lock. That's the way it usually is in high-rises. A doorman, however slipshod he may be, endows tenants with a sense of security. The residents of un-serviced walk-ups affix three or four extra locks to their doors and still cower behind them.

The apartment had an unfinished air about it, and I sensed that Paula had lived there for a few months without making the place her own. There were no rugs on the wood parquet floor. The walls were decorated with a few unframed posters held up by scraps of red Mystik tape. The apartment was an L-shaped studio with a platform bed occupying the foot of the L. There were newspapers and magazines scattered around the place but no books. I noticed copies of *Variety* and *Rolling Stone* and *People* and *The Village Voice*.

The television set was a tiny Sony perched on top of a chest of drawers. There was no stereo, but there were a few dozen records, mostly classical with a sprinkling of folk music, Pete Seeger and Joan Baez and Dave Van Ronk. There was a dust-free rectangle on top of the dresser next to the Sony.

I looked through the drawers and closets. A lot of Paula's clothes. I recognized some of the outfits, or thought I did.

Someone had closed the window. There were two windows that opened, one in the sleeping alcove, the other in the living room section, but a row of undisturbed potted plants in front of the bedroom window made it evident she'd gone out of the other one. I wondered why anyone had bothered to close it. In case of rain, I supposed. That was only sensible. But I suspect the gesture must have been less calculated than that, a reflexive act akin to tugging a sheet over the face of a corpse.

I went into the bathroom. A killer could have hidden in the stall shower. If there'd been a killer.

Why was I still thinking in terms of a killer?

I checked the medicine cabinet. There were little tubes and vials of cosmetics, though only a handful compared with the array on one of the bedside tables. Here were containers of aspirin and other headache remedies, a tube of antibiotic ointment, several prescriptions and nonprescription hay fever preparations, a cardboard packet of Band-Aids, a roll of adhesive tape, a box of gauze pads. Some Q-tips, a hairbrush, a couple of combs. A toothbrush in the holder.

There were no footprints on the floor of the stall shower. Of course he could have been barefoot. Or he could have run water and washed away the traces of his presence before he left.

I went over and examined the windowsill. I hadn't asked Guzik if they'd dusted for prints and I was reasonably certain no one had bothered. I wouldn't have taken the trouble in their position. I couldn't learn anything looking at the sill. I opened the window a foot or so and stuck my head out, but when I looked down the vertigo was extremely unpleasant and I drew my head back inside at once. I left the window open, though. The room could stand a change of air.

There were four folding chairs in the room, two of them closed and leaning against a wall, one near the bed, the fourth alongside the window. They were royal blue and made of high-impact plastic. The one by the window had her clothes piled on it. I went through the stack. She'd placed them deliberately on the chair but hadn't bothered folding them.

You never know what suicides will do. One man will put on a tuxedo before blowing his brains out. Another one will take off everything. Naked I came into the world and naked will I go out of it, something like that.

A skirt. Beneath it a pair of panty hose. Then a blouse, and under it a bra with two small, lightly padded cups, I put the clothing back as I had found it, feeling like a violator of the dead.

The bed was unmade. I sat on the edge of it and looked across the room at a poster of Mick Jagger. I don't know how long I sat there. Ten minutes, maybe.

On the way out I looked at the chain bolt. I hadn't even noticed it when I came in. The chain had been neatly severed. Half of it was still in the slot on the door while the other half hung from its mounting on the jamb. I closed the door and fitted the two halves together, then released them and let them dangle. Then I touched their ends together again. I unhooked the end of the chain from the slot and went to the bathroom for the roll of adhesive tape. I brought the tape back with me, tore off a piece, and used it to fasten the chain back together again. Then I let myself out of the apartment and tried to engage the chain bolt from outside, but the tape slipped whenever I put any pressure on it.

I went inside again and studied the chain bolt. I

decided I was behaving erratically, that Paula Wittlauer had gone out the window of her own accord. I looked at the windowsill again. The light dusting of soot didn't tell me anything one way or the other. New York's air is filthy and the accumulation of soot could have been deposited in a couple of hours, even with the window shut. It didn't mean anything.

I looked at the heap of clothes on the chair, and I looked again at the chain bolt, and I rode the elevator to the basement and found either the superintendent or one of his assistants. I asked to borrow a screwdriver. He gave me a long screwdriver with an amber plastic grip. He didn't ask me who I was or what I wanted it for.

I returned to Paula Wittlauer's apartment and removed the chain bolt from its moorings on the door and jamb. I left the building and walked around the corner to a hardware store on Ninth Avenue. They had a good selection of chain bolts but I wanted one identical to the one I'd removed and I had to walk down Ninth Avenue as far as Fiftieth Street and check four stores before I found what I was looking for.

Back in Paula's apartment I mounted the new chain bolt, using the holes in which the original had been mounted. I tightened the screws with the super's screwdriver and stood out in the corridor and played with the chain. My hands are large and not terribly skillful, but even so I was able to lock and unlock the chain bolt from outside the apartment.

I don't know who put it up, Paula or a previous tenant or someone on the building staff, but that chain bolt had been as much protection as the Sanitized wrapper on a motel toilet seat. As evidence that Paula'd been alone when she went out the window, well, it wasn't worth a thing.

I replaced the original chain bolt, put the new one in

my pocket, returned to the elevator, and gave back the screwdriver. The man I returned it to seemed surprised to get it back.

It took me a couple of hours to find Cary McCloud. I'd learned that he tended bar evenings at a club in the West Village called The Spider's Web. I got down there around five. The guy behind the bar had knobby wrists and an underslung jaw and he wasn't Cary McCloud. "He don't come on till eight," he told me, "and he's off tonight anyway." I asked where I could find McCloud. "Sometimes he's here afternoons but he ain't been in today. As far as where you could look for him, that I couldn't tell you."

A lot of people couldn't tell me but eventually I ran across someone who could. You can quit the police force but you can't stop looking and sounding like a cop, and while that's a hindrance in some situations it's a help in others. Ultimately I found a man in a bar down the block from The Spider's Web who'd learned it was best to cooperate with the police if it didn't cost you anything. He gave me an address on Barrow Street and told me which bell to ring.

I went to the building but I rang several other bells until somebody buzzed me through the downstairs door. I didn't want Cary to know he had company coming. I climbed two flights of stairs to the apartment he was supposed to be occupying. The bell downstairs hadn't had his name on it. It hadn't had any name at all.

Loud rock music was coming through his door. I stood in front of it for a minute, then hammered on it loud enough to make myself heard over the electric guitars. After a moment the music dropped in volume. I pounded on the door again and a male voice asked who I was.

I said, "Police. Open up." That's a misdemeanor but I didn't expect to get in trouble for it.

"What's it about?"

"Open up, McCloud."

"Oh, Jesus," he said. He sounded tired, aggravated. "How did you find me, anyway? Give me a minute, huh? I want to put some clothes on."

Sometimes that's what they say while they're putting a clip into an automatic. Then they pump a handful of shots through the door and into you if you're still standing behind it. But his voice didn't have that kind of edge to it and I couldn't summon up enough anxiety to get out of the way. Instead I put my ear against the door and heard whispering within. I couldn't make out what they were whispering about or get any sense of the person who was with him. The music was down in volume but there was still enough of it to cover their conversation.

The door opened. He was tall and thin, with hollow cheeks and prominent eyebrows and a worn, wasted look to him. He must have been in his early thirties and he didn't really look much older than that but you sensed that in another ten years he'd look twenty years older. If he lived that long. He wore patched jeans and a T-shirt with The Spider's Web silkscreened on it. Beneath the legend there was a sketch of a web. A macho spider stood at one end of it, grinning, extending two of his eight arms to welcome a hesitant girlish fly.

He noticed me noticing the shirt and managed a grin. "Place where I work," he said.

"I know."

"So come into my parlor. It ain't much but it's home."

I followed him inside, drew the door shut after me.

The room was about fifteen feet square and held nothing you could call furniture. There was a mattress on the floor in one corner and a couple of cardboard cartons alongside it. The music was coming from a stereo, turntable and tuner and two speakers all in a row along the far wall. There was a closed door over on the right. I figured it led to the bathroom, and that there was a woman on the other side of it.

"I guess this is about Paula," he said. I nodded. "I been over this with you guys," he said. "I was nowhere near there when it happened. The last I saw her was five, six hours before she killed herself. I was working at the Web and she came down and sat at the bar. I gave her a couple of drinks and she split."

"And you went on working."

"Until I closed up. I kicked everybody out a little after three and it was close to four by the time I had the place swept up and the garbage on the street and the window gates locked. Then I came over here and picked up Sunny and we went up to the place on Fifty-third."

"And you got there when?"

"Hell, I don't know. I wear a watch but I don't look at it every damn minute. I suppose it took five minutes to walk here and then Sunny and I hopped right in a cab and we were at Patsy's in ten minutes at the outside, that's the after-hours place, I told you people all of this, I really wish you would talk to each other and leave me the hell alone."

"Why doesn't Sunny come out and tell me about it?" I nodded at the bathroom door. "Maybe she can remember the time a little more clearly."

"Sunny? She stepped out a little while ago."

"She's not in the bathroom?"

"Nope. Nobody's in the bathroom."

"Mind if I see for myself?"

"Not if you can show me a warrant."

We looked at each other. I told him I figured I could take his word for it. He said he could always be trusted to tell the truth. I said I sensed as much about him.

He said, "What's the hassle, huh? I know you guys got forms to fill out, but why not give me a break? She killed herself and I wasn't anywhere near her when it happened."

He could have been. The times were vague, and whoever Sunny turned out to be, the odds were good that she'd have no more time sense than a koala bear. There were any number of ways he could have found a few minutes to go up to Fifty-seventh Street and heave Paula out a window, but it didn't add up that way and he just didn't feel like a killer to me. I knew what Ruth meant and I agreed with her that he was capable of murder but I don't think he'd been capable of this particular murder.

I said, "When did you go back to the apartment?"

"Who said I did?"

"You picked up your clothes, Cary."

"That was yesterday afternoon. The hell, I needed my clothes and stuff."

"How long were you living there?"

He hedged. "I wasn't exactly living there."

"Where were you exactly living?"

"I wasn't exactly living anywhere. I kept most of my stuff at Paula's place and I stayed with her most of the time but it wasn't as serious as actual living together. We were both too loose for anything like that. Anyway, the thing with Paula, it was pretty much winding itself down. She was a little too crazy for me." He smiled with his mouth. "They have to be a little crazy," he said, "but when they're too crazy it gets to be too much of a hassle."

Oh, he could have killed her. He could kill anyone if he had to, if someone was making too much of a hassle. But if he were to kill cleverly, faking the suicide in such an artful fashion, fastening the chain bolt on his way out, he'd pick a time when he had a solid alibi. He was not the sort to be so precise and so slipshod all at the same time.

"So you went and picked up your stuff."

"Right."

"Including the stereo and records."

"The stereo was mine. The records, I left the folk music and the classical shit because that belonged to Paula. I just took my records."

"And the stereo."

"Right."

"You got a bill of sale for it, I suppose."

"Who keeps that crap?"

"What if I said Paula kept the bill of sale? What if I said it was in with her papers and canceled checks?"

"You're fishing."

"You sure of that?"

"Nope. But if you did say that, I suppose I'd say the stereo was a gift from her to me. You're not really gonna charge me with stealing a stereo, are you?"

"Why should I? Robbing the dead's a sacred tradition. You took the drugs, too, didn't you? Her medicine cabinet used to look like a drugstore but there was nothing stronger than Excedrin when I took a look. That's why Sunny's in the bathroom. If I hit the door all the pretty little pills go down the toilet."

"I guess you can think that if you want."

"And I can come back with a warrant if I want."

"That's the idea."

"I ought to rap on the door just to do you out of the drugs but it doesn't seem worth the trouble. That's Paula Wittlauer's stereo. I suppose it's worth a couple hundred dollars. And you're not her heir. Unplug that thing and wrap it up, McCloud. I'm taking it with me."

"The hell you are."

"The hell I'm not."

"You want to take anything but your own ass out of here, you come back with a warrant. Then we'll talk about it."

"I don't need a warrant."

"You can't — "

"I don't need a warrant because I'm not a cop. I'm a detective, McCloud, I'm private, and I'm working for Ruth Wittlauer, and that's who's getting the stereo. I don't know if she wants it or not, but that's her problem. She doesn't want Paula's pills so you can pop them yourself or give them to your girlfriend. You can shove 'em up your ass for all I care. But I'm walking out of here with that stereo and I'll walk through you if I have to, and don't think I wouldn't enjoy it."

"You're not even a cop."

"Right."

"You got no authority at all." He spoke in tones of wonder. "You said you were a cop."

"You can always sue me."

"You can't take that stereo. You can't even be in this room."

"That's right." I was itching for him. I could feel my blood in my veins. "I'm bigger than you," I said, "and I'm a whole lot harder, and I'd get a certain amount of satisfaction in beating the crap out of you. I don't like you. It bothers me that you didn't kill her because somebody did and it would be a pleasure to hang it on you. But you didn't do it. Unplug the stereo and pack it up so I can carry it or I'm going to take you apart."

I meant it and he realized as much. He thought about taking a shot at me and he decided it wasn't worth it. Maybe it wasn't all that much of a stereo. While he was unhooking it I dumped a carton of his clothes on the floor and we packed the stereo in it. On my way out the door he said he could always go to the cops and tell them what I'd done.

"I don't think you want to do that," I said.

"You said somebody killed her."

"That's right."

"You just making noise?"

"No."

"You're serious?" I nodded. "She didn't kill herself? I thought it was open and shut, from what the cops said. It's interesting. In a way, I guess you could say it's a load off my mind."

"How do you figure that?"

He shrugged. "I thought, you know, maybe she was upset it wasn't working out between us. At the Web the vibes were on the heavy side, if you follow me. Our thing was falling apart and I was seeing Sunny and she was seeing other guys and I thought maybe that was what did it for her. I suppose I blamed myself, like."

"I can see it was eating away at you."

"I just said it was on my mind."

I didn't say anything.

"Man," he said, "*nothing* eats away at me. You let things get to you that way and it's death."

I shouldered the carton and headed on down the stairs.

Ruth Wittlauer had supplied me with an Irving Place address and a GRamercy 5 telephone number. I called the number and didn't get an answer, so I walked over to Hudson and caught a northbound cab. There were no messages for me at the hotel desk. I put Paula's stereo in my room, tried Ruth's number again, then walked over to the Eighteenth Precinct. Guzik had gone off duty but the desk man told me to try a restaurant around the corner, and I found him there drinking draft Heinekens with another cop, named Birnbaum. I sat at their table and ordered bourbon for myself and another round for the two of them.

I said, "I have a favor to ask. I'd like you to seal Paula Wittlauer's apartment."

"We closed that out," Guzik reminded me.

"I know, and the boyfriend closed out the dead girl's stereo." I told him how I'd reclaimed the unit from Cary McCloud. "I'm working for Ruth, Paula's sister. The least I can do is make sure she gets what's coming to her. She's not up to cleaning out the apartment now and it's rented through the first of October. McCloud's got a key and God knows how many other people have keys. If you slap a seal on the door it'd keep the grave robbers away."

"I guess we can do that. Tomorrow all right?"

"Tonight would be better."

"What's there to steal? You got the stereo out of there and I didn't see anything else around that was worth much."

"Things have a sentimental value."

He eyed me, frowned. "I'll make a phone call," he said. He went to the booth in the back and I jawed with Birnbaum until he came back and told me it was all taken care of.

I said, "Another thing I was wondering. You must have had a photographer on the scene. Somebody to take pictures of the body and all that."

"Sure. That's routine."

"Did he go up to the apartment while he was at it? Take a roll of interior shots?"

"Yeah. Why?"

"I thought maybe I could have a look at them."

"What for?"

"You never know. The reason I knew it was Paula's stereo in McCloud's apartment was I could see the pattern in the dust on top of the dresser where it had been. If you've got interior pictures maybe I'll see something else that's not there anymore and I can lean on McCloud a little and recover it for my client."

"And that's why you'd like to see the pictures."

"Right."

He gave me a look. "That door was bolted from the inside, Matt. With a chain bolt."

"I know."

"And there was no one in the apartment when we went in there."

"I know that, too."

"You're still barking up the murder tree, aren't you? Jesus, the case is closed and the reason it's closed is the ditzy broad killed herself. What are you making waves for?"

"I'm not. I just wanted to see the pictures."

"To see if somebody stole her diaphragm or something."

"Something like that." I drank what remained of my drink. "You need a new hat anyway, Guzik. The weather's turning and a fellow like you needs a hat for fall."

"If I had the price of a hat, maybe I'd go out and get one."

"You got it," I said.

He nodded and we told Birnbaum we wouldn't be long. I walked with Guzik around the corner to the Eighteenth. On the way I palmed him two tens and a five, twenty-five dollars, the price of a hat in police parlance. He made the bills disappear.

I waited at his desk while he pulled the Paula Wittlauer file. There were about a dozen black-and-white prints, eight by tens, high-contrast glossies. Perhaps half of them showed Paula's corpse from various angles. I had no interest in these but I made myself look at them as a sort of reinforcement, so I wouldn't forget what I was doing on the case.

The other pictures were interior shots of the L-shaped apartment. I noted the wide-open window, the dresser with the stereo sitting on it, the chair with her clothing piled haphazardly upon it. I separated the interior pictures from the ones showing the corpse and told Guzik I wanted to keep them for the time being. He didn't mind.

He cocked his head and looked at me. "You got something, Matt?"

"Nothing worth talking about."

"If you ever do, I'll want to hear about it."

"Sure."

"You like the life you're leading? Working private, scuffling around?"

"It seems to suit me."

He thought it over, nodded. Then he started for the stairs and I followed after him.

Later that evening I managed to reach Ruth Wittlauer. I bundled the stereo into a cab and took it to her place. She lived in a well-kept brownstone a block and a half from Gramercy Park. Her apartment was inexpensively furnished but the pieces looked to have been chosen with care. The place was clean and neat. Her clock radio was tuned to an FM station that was playing chamber music. She had coffee made and I accepted a cup and sipped it while I told her about recovering the stereo from Cary McCloud.

"I wasn't sure whether you could use it," I said, "but I couldn't see any reason why he should keep it. You can always sell it."

"No, I'll keep it. I just have a twenty-dollar record player that I bought on Fourteenth Street. Paula's stereo cost a couple of hundred dollars." She managed a smile.

"So you've already more than earned what I gave you. Did he kill her?"

"No."

"You're sure of that?"

I nodded. "He'd kill if he had a reason but I don't think he did. And if he did kill her he'd never have taken the stereo or the drugs, and he wouldn't have acted the way he did. There was never a moment when I had the feeling that he'd killed her. And you have to follow your instincts in this kind of situation. Once they point things out to you, then you can usually find the facts to go with them."

"And you're sure my sister killed herself?"

"No. I'm pretty sure someone gave her a hand."

Her eyes widened.

I said, "It's mostly intuition. But there are a few facts to support it." I told her about the chain bolt, how it had proved to the police that Paula'd killed herself, how my experiment had shown it could have been fastened from the corridor. Ruth got very excited at this but I explained that it didn't prove anything in and of itself, only that suicide remained a theoretical possibility.

Then I showed her the pictures I'd obtained from Guzik. I selected one shot which showed the chair with Paula's clothing without showing too much of the window. I didn't want to make Ruth look at the window.

"The chair," I said, pointing to it. "I noticed this when I was in your sister's apartment. I wanted to see a photograph taken at the time to make sure things hadn't been rearranged by the cops or McCloud or somebody else. But that clothing's exactly the way it was when I saw it."

"I don't understand."

"The supposition is that Paula got undressed, put her clothes on the chair, then went to the window and jumped." Her lip was trembling but she was holding herself together and I went right on talking. "Or she'd taken her clothes off earlier and maybe she took a shower or a nap and then came back and jumped. But look at the chair. She didn't fold her clothes neatly, she didn't put them away. And she didn't just drop them on the floor, either. I'm no authority on the way women get undressed but I don't think many people would do it that way."

Ruth nodded. Her face was thoughtful.

"That wouldn't mean very much by itself. If she were upset or stoned or confused she might have thrown things on the chair as she took them off. But that's not what happened. The order of the clothing is all wrong. The bra's underneath the blouse, the panty hose is underneath the skirt. She took her bra off after she took her blouse off, obviously, so it should have wound up on top of the blouse, not under it."

"Of course."

I held up a hand. "It's nothing like proof, Ruth. There are any number of other explanations. Maybe she knocked the stuff onto the floor and then picked it up and the order of the garments got switched around. Maybe one of the cops went through the clothing before the photographer came around with his camera. I don't really have anything terribly strong to go on."

"But you think she was murdered."

"Yes, I guess I do."

"That's what I thought all along. Of course I had a reason to think so."

"Maybe I've got one, too. I don't know."

"What are you going to do now?"

"I think I'll poke around a little. I don't know much about Paula's life. I'll have to learn more if I'm going to find out who killed her. But it's up to you to decide whether you want me to stay with it."

"Of course I do. Why wouldn't I?"

"Because it probably won't lead anywhere. Suppose she was upset after her conversation with McCloud and she picked up a stranger and took him home with her and he killed her. If that's the case we'll never know who he was."

"You're going to stay with it, aren't you?"

"I suppose I want to."

"It'll be complicated, though. It'll take you some time. I suppose you'll want more money." Her gaze was very direct. "I gave you two hundred dollars. I have three hundred more that I can afford to pay. I don't mind paying it, Mr. Scudder. I already got . . . I got my money's worth for the first two hundred, didn't I? The stereo. When the three hundred runs out, well, you can tell me if you think it's worth staying with the case. I couldn't afford more cash right away, but I could arrange to pay you later on or something like that."

I shook my head. "It won't come to more than that," I said. "No matter how much time I spend on it. And you keep the three hundred for the time being, all right? I'll take it from you later on. If I need it, and if I've earned it."

"That doesn't seem right."

"It seems right to me," I said. "And don't make the mistake of thinking I'm being charitable."

"But your time's valuable."

I shook my head. "Not to me it isn't."

I spent the next five days picking the scabs off Paula Wittlauer's life. It kept turning out to be a waste of time but the time's always gone before you realize you've wasted it. And I'd been telling the truth when I said my time wasn't valuable. I had nothing better to do, and my peeks into the corners of Paula's world kept me busy.

Her life involved more than a saloon on Ninth Avenue and an apartment on Fifty-seventh Street, more than serving drinks and sharing a bed with Cary McCloud. She did other things. She went one evening a week to group therapy on West Seventy-ninth Street. She took voice lessons every Tuesday morning on Amsterdam Avenue. She had an ex-boyfriend she saw once in a while. She hung out in a couple of bars in the neighborhood and a couple of others in the Village. She did this, she did that, she went here, she went there, and I kept busy dragging myself around town and talking to all sorts of people, and I managed to learn quite a bit about the person she'd been and the life she'd led without learning anything at all about the person who'd put her on the pavement.

At the same time, I tried to track her movements on the final night of her life. She'd evidently gone more or less directly to The Spider's Web after finishing her shift at Armstrong's. Maybe she'd stopped at her apartment for a shower and a change of clothes, but without further ado she'd headed downtown. Somewhere around ten she left the Web, and I traced her from there to a couple of other Village bars. She hadn't stayed at either of them long, taking a quick drink or two and moving on. She'd left alone as far as anyone seemed to remember. This didn't prove a thing because she could have stopped elsewhere before continuing uptown, or she could have picked someone up on the street, which I'd learned was something she'd done more than once in her young life. She could have found her killer loitering on a street corner or she could have phoned him and arranged to meet him at her apartment.

Her apartment. The doormen changed off at midnight, but it was impossible to determine whether she'd returned before or after the changing of the guard. She'd lived there, she was a regular tenant, and when she entered or left the building it was not a noteworthy occasion. It was something she did every night, so when she came home for the final time the man at the door had no reason to know it was the final time and thus no reason to take mental notes.

Had she come in alone or with a companion? No one could say, which did suggest that she'd come in alone. If she'd been with someone her entrance would have been a shade more memorable. But this also proved nothing, because I stood on the other side of Fifty-seventh Street one night and watched the doorway of her building, and the doorman didn't take the pride in his position that the afternoon doorman had shown. He was away from the door almost as often as he was on it.

She could have walked in flanked by six Turkish sailors and there was a chance no one would have seen her.

The doorman who'd been on duty when she went out the window was a rheumy-eyed Irishman with liver-spotted hands. He hadn't actually seen her land. He'd been in the lobby, keeping himself out of the wind, and then he came rushing out when he heard the impact of the body on the street.

He couldn't get over the sound she made.

"All of a sudden there was this noise," he said. "Just out of the blue there was this noise and it must be it's my imagination but I swear I felt it in my feet. I swear she shook the earth. I had no idea what it was, and then I came rushing out, and Jesus God, there she was."

"Didn't you hear a scream?"

"Street was empty just then. This side, anyway. Nobody around to scream."

"Didn't *she* scream on the way down?"

"Did somebody say she screamed? I never heard it."

Do people scream as they fall? They generally do in films and on television. During my days on the force I saw several of them after they jumped, and by the time I got to them there were no screams echoing in the air. And a few times I'd been on hand while they talked someone in off a ledge, but in each instance the talking was successful and I didn't have to watch a falling body accelerate according to the immutable laws of physics.

Could you get much of a scream out in four seconds?

I stood in the street where she'd fallen and I looked up toward her window. I counted off four seconds in my mind. A voice shrieked in my brain. It was Thursday night, actually Friday morning, one o'clock. Time I got myself around the corner to Armstrong's, because in another couple of hours Justin would be closing for the night and I'd want to be drunk enough to sleep.

And an hour or so after that she'd be one week dead.

I'd worked myself into a reasonably bleak mood by the time I got to Armstrong's. I skipped the coffee and crawled straight into the bourbon bottle, and before long it began to do what it was supposed to do. It blurred the corners of the mind so I couldn't see the bad dark things that lurked there.

When Trina finished for the night she joined me and I bought her a couple of drinks. I don't remember what we talked about. Some but by no means all of our conversation touched upon Paula Wittlauer. Trina hadn't known Paula terribly well — their contact had been largely limited to the two hours a day when their shifts overlapped — but she knew a little about the sort of life Paula had been leading. There'd been a year or two when her own life had not been terribly different from Paula's. Now she had things more or less under control, and maybe there would have come a time when Paula would have taken charge of her life, but that was something we'd never know now.

I suppose it was close to three when I walked Trina home. Our conversation had turned thoughtful and reflective. On the street she said it was a lousy night for being alone. I thought of high windows and evil shapes in dark corners and took her hand in mine.

She lives on Fifty-sixth between Ninth and Tenth. While we waited for the light to change at Fifty-seventh Street I looked over at Paula's building. We were far enough away to look at the high floors. Only a couple of windows were lighted.

That was when I got it.

I've never understood how people think of things, how little perceptions trigger greater insights. Thoughts just seem to come to me. I had it now, and something clicked within me and a source of tension unwound itself.

I said something to that effect to Trina.

"You know who killed her?"

"Not exactly," I said. "But I know how to find out. And it can wait until tomorrow."

The light changed and we crossed the street.

She was still sleeping when I left. I got out of bed and dressed in silence, then let myself out of her apartment. I had some coffee and a toasted English muffin at the Red Flame. Then I went across the street to Paula's building. I started on the tenth floor and worked my way up, checking the three or four possible apartments on each floor. A lot of people weren't home. I worked my way clear to the top floor, the twenty-fourth, and by the time I was done I had three possibles listed in my notebook and a list of over a dozen apartments I'd have to check that evening.

At eight-thirty that night I rang the bell of Apartment 21G. It was directly in line with Paula's apartment and four flights above it. The man who answered the bell wore a pair of Lee corduroy slacks and a shirt with a blue vertical stripe on a white background. His socks were dark blue and he wasn't wearing shoes.

I said, "I want to talk with you about Paula Wittlauer."

His face fell apart and I forgot my three possibles forever because he was the man I wanted. He just stood there. I pushed the door open and stepped forward and he moved back automatically to make room for me. I drew the door shut after me and walked around him, crossing the room to the window. There wasn't a speck of dust or soot on the sill. It was immaculate, as well-scrubbed as Lady Macbeth's hands.

I turned to him. His name was Lane Posmantur and I suppose he was around forty, thickening at the waist, his dark hair starting to go thin on top. His glasses were thick and it was hard to read his eyes through them but it didn't matter. I didn't need to see his eyes.

"She went out this window," I said. "Didn't she?"

"I don't know what you're talking about."

"Do you want to know what triggered it for me, Mr. Posmantur? I was thinking of all the things nobody noticed. No one saw her enter the building. Neither doorman remembered it because it wasn't something they'd be likely to remember. Nobody saw her go out the window. The cops had to look for an open window in order to know who the hell she was. They backtracked her from the window she fell out of.

"And nobody saw the killer leave the building. Now that's the one thing that would have been noticed, and that's the point that occurred to me. It wasn't that significant by itself but it made me dig a little deeper. The doorman was alert once her body hit the street. He'd remember who went in or out of the building from that point on. So it occurred to me that maybe the killer was still inside the building, and then I got the idea that she was killed by someone who *lived* in the building, and from that point on it was just a question of finding you because all of a sudden it all made sense."

I told him about the clothes on the chair. "She didn't take them off and pile them up like that. Her killer put her clothes like that, and he dumped them on the chair so that it would look as though she undressed in her apartment, and so that it would be assumed she'd gone out of her own window.

"But she went out of your window, didn't she?"

He looked at me. After a moment he said he thought he'd better sit down. He went to an armchair and sat in it. I stayed on my feet.

I said, "She came here. I guess she took off her clothes and you went to bed with her. Is that right?"

He hesitated, then nodded.

"What made you decide to kill her?"

"I didn't."

I looked at him. He looked away, then met my gaze, then avoided my eyes again. "Tell me about it," I suggested. He looked away again and a minute went by and then he started to talk.

It was about what I'd figured. She was living with Cary McCloud but she and Lane Posmantur would get together now and then for a quickie. He was a lab technician at Roosevelt and he brought home drugs from time to time and perhaps that was part of his attraction for her. She'd turned up that night a little after two and they went to bed. She was really flying, he said, and he'd been taking pills himself, it was something he'd begun doing lately, maybe seeing her had something to do with it.

They went to bed and did the dirty deed, and then maybe they slept for an hour, something like that, and then she was awake and coming unglued, getting really hysterical, and he tried to settle her down and he gave her a couple of slaps to bring her around, except they didn't bring her around, and she was staggering and she tripped over the coffee table and fell funny, and by the time he sorted himself out and went to her she was lying with her head at a crazy angle and he knew her neck was broken and when he tried for a pulse there was no pulse to be found.

"All I could think of was she was dead in my apartment and full of drugs and I was in trouble."

"So you put her out the window."

"I was going to take her back to her own apartment. I started to dress her but it was impossible. And even with her clothes on I couldn't risk running into somebody in the hallway or on the elevator. It was crazy.

"I left her here and went to her apartment. I thought maybe Cary would help me. I rang the bell and nobody answered and I used her key and the chain bolt was on. Then I remembered she used to fasten it from outside. She'd showed me how she could do that. I tried with mine but it was installed properly and there's not enough play in the chain. I unhooked her bolt and went inside.

"Then I got the idea. I went back to my apartment and got her clothes and I rushed back and put them on her chair. I opened her window wide. On my way out the door I put her lights on and hooked the chain bolt again.

"I came back here to my own apartment. I took her pulse again and she was dead, she hadn't moved or anything, and I couldn't do anything for her, all I could do was stay out of it, and I, I turned off the lights here, and I opened my own window and dragged her body over to it, and, oh, God in heaven, God, I almost couldn't make myself do it but it was an accident that she was dead and I was so damned *afraid* — "

"And you dropped her out and closed the window."

He nodded. "And if her neck was broken it was something that happened in the fall. And whatever drugs were in her system was just something she'd taken by herself, and they'd never do an autopsy anyway. And you were home free."

"I didn't hurt her," he said. "I was just protecting myself."

"Do you really believe that, Lane?"

"What do you mean?"

"You're not a doctor. Maybe she was dead when you threw her out the window. Maybe she wasn't."

"There was no pulse!"

"You couldn't find a pulse. That doesn't mean there wasn't any. Did you try artificial respiration? Do you know if there was any brain activity? No, of course not. All you know was that you looked for a pulse and you couldn't find one."

"Her neck was broken."

"Maybe. How many broken necks have you had occasion to diagnose? And people sometimes break their necks and live anyway. The point is that you couldn't have known she was dead and you were too worried about your own skin to do what you should have done. You should have phoned for an ambulance. You know that's what you should have done and you knew it at the time but you wanted to stay out of it. I've known junkies who left their buddies to die of overdoses because they didn't want to get involved. You went them one better. You put her out a window and let her fall twenty-one stories so that you wouldn't get involved, and for all you know she was alive when you let go of her."

"No," he said. "No. She was dead."

I'd told Ruth Wittlauer she could wind up believing whatever she wanted. People believe what they want to believe. It was just as true for Lane Posmantur.

"Maybe she was dead," I said. "Maybe that's your fault, too."

"What do you mean?"

"You said you slapped her to bring her around. What kind of a slap, Lane?"

"I just tapped her on the face."

"Just a brisk slap to straighten her out."

"That's right."

"Oh, hell, Lane. Who knows how hard you hit her? Who knows whether you may not have given her a shove? She wasn't the only one on pills. You said she was flying. Well, I think maybe you were doing a little flying yourself. And you'd been sleepy and you were groggy and she was buzzing around the room and being a general pain in the ass, and you gave her a slap and a shove and another slap and another shove and — "

"No!"

"And she fell down."

"It was an accident."

"It always is."

"I didn't hurt her. I liked her. She was a good kid, we got on fine, I didn't hurt her, I—"

"Put your shoes on, Lane."

"What for?"

"I'm taking you to the police station. It's a few blocks from here, not very far at all."

"Am I under arrest?"

"I'm not a policeman." I'd never gotten around to saying who I was and he'd never thought to ask. "My name's Scudder, I'm working for Paula's sister. I suppose you're under citizen's arrest. I want you to come to the precinct house with me. There's a cop named Guzik there and you can talk to him."

"I don't have to say anything," he said. He thought for a moment. "You're not a cop."

"No."

"What I said to you doesn't mean a thing." He took a breath, straightened up a little in his chair. "You can't prove a thing," he said. "Not a thing."

"Maybe I can and maybe I can't. You probably left prints in Paula's apartment. I had them seal the place a while ago and maybe they'll find traces of your presence. I don't know if Paula left any prints here or not. You probably scrubbed them up. But there may be neighbors who know you were sleeping with her, and someone may have noticed you scampering back and forth between the apartments that night, and it's even possible a neighbor heard the two of you struggling in here just before she went out the window. When the cops know what to look for, Lane, they usually find it sooner or later. It's knowing what you're after that's the hard part.

"But that's not even the point. Put your shoes on, Lane. That's right. Now we're going to go see Guzik, that's his name, and he's going to advise you of your rights. He'll tell you that you have a right to remain silent, and that's the truth, Lane, that's a right that you have. And if you remain silent and if you get a decent lawyer and do what he tells you I think you can beat this charge, Lane. I really do."

"Why are you telling me this?"

"Why?" I was starting to feel tired, drained, but I kept on with it. "Because the worst thing you could do is remain silent, Lane. Believe me, that's the worst thing you could do. If you're smart you'll tell Guzik everything you remember. You'll make a complete voluntary statement and you'll read it over when they type it up and you'll sign your name on the bottom.

"Because you're not really a killer, Lane. It doesn't come easily to you. If Cary McCloud had killed her he'd never lose a night's sleep over it. But you're not a sociopath. You were drugged and half-crazy and terrified and you did something wrong and it's eating you up. Your face fell apart the minute I walked in here tonight.

You could play it cute and beat this charge, Lane, but all you'd wind up doing is beating yourself.

"Because you live on a high floor, Lane, and the ground's only four seconds away. And if you squirm off the hook you'll never get it out of your head, you'll never be able to mark it Paid in Full, and one day or night you'll open the window and you'll go out of it, Lane. You'll remember the sound her body made when she hit the street — "

"*No!*"

I took his arm. "Come on," I said. "We'll go see Guzik."

A CANDLE FOR THE BAG LADY

He was a thin young man in a blue pinstripe suit. His shirt was white with a button-down collar. His glasses had oval lenses in brown tortoiseshell frames. His hair was a dark brown, short but not severely so, neatly combed, parted on the right. I saw him come in and watched him ask a question at the bar. Billie was working afternoons that week. I watched as he nodded at the young man, then swung his sleepy eyes over in my direction. I lowered my own eyes and looked at a cup of coffee laced with bourbon while the fellow walked over to my table.

"Matthew Scudder?" I looked up at him, nodded. "I'm Aaron Creighton. I looked for you at your hotel. The fellow on the desk told me I might find you here."

Here was Armstrong's, a Ninth Avenue saloon around the corner from my Fifty-seventh Street hotel. The lunch crowd was gone except for a couple of stragglers in front whose voices were starting to thicken with alcohol. The streets outside were full of May sunshine. The winter had been cold and deep and long. I couldn't recall a more welcome spring.

"I called you a couple times last week, Mr. Scudder. I guess you didn't get my messages."

I'd gotten two of them and ignored them, not knowing who he was or what he wanted and unwilling to spend a dime for the answer. But I went along with the fiction. "It's a cheap hotel," I said. "They're not always too good about messages."

"I can imagine. Uh. Is there someplace we can talk?"

"How about right here?"

He looked around. I don't suppose he was used to conducting his business in bars but he evidently decided it would be all right to make an exception. He set his briefcase on the floor and seated himself across the table from me. Angela, the new day-shift waitress, hurried over to get his order. He glanced at my cup and said he'd have coffee, too.

"I'm an attorney," he said. My first thought was that he didn't look like a lawyer, but then I realized he probably dealt with civil cases. My experience as a cop had given me a lot of experience with criminal lawyers. The breed ran to several types, none of them his.

I waited for him to tell me why he wanted to hire me. But he crossed me up.

"I'm handling an estate," he said, and paused, and gave what seemed a calculated if well-intentioned smile. "It's my pleasant duty to tell you you've come into a small legacy, Mr. Scudder."

"Someone's left me money?"

"Twelve hundred dollars."

Who could have died? I'd lost touch long since with any of my relatives. My parents went years ago and we'd never been close with the rest of the family.

I said, "Who — ?"

"Mary Alice Redfield."

I repeated the name aloud. It was not entirely unfamiliar but I had no idea who Mary Alice Redfield might be. I looked at Aaron Creighton. I couldn't make out his eyes behind the glasses but there was a smile's ghost on his thin lips, as if my reaction was not unexpected.

"She's dead?"

"Almost three months ago."

"I didn't know her."

"She knew you. You probably knew her, Mr. Scudder. Perhaps you didn't know her by name." His smile deepened. Angela had brought his coffee. He stirred milk and sugar into it, took a careful sip, nodded his approval. "Miss Redfield was murdered." He said this as if he'd had practice uttering a phrase which did not come naturally to him. "She was killed quite brutally in late February for no apparent reason, another innocent victim of street crime."

"She lived in New York?"

"Oh, yes. In this neighborhood."

"And she was killed around here?"

"On West Fifty-fifth Street between Ninth and Tenth avenues. Her body was found in an alleyway. She'd been stabbed repeatedly and strangled with the scarf she had been wearing."

Late February. Mary Alice Redfield. West Fifty-fifth between Ninth and Tenth. Murder most foul. Stabbed and strangled, a dead woman in an alleyway. I usually kept track of murders, perhaps out of a vestige of professionalism, perhaps because I couldn't cease to be fascinated by man's inhumanity to man. Mary Alice Redfield had willed me twelve hundred dollars. And someone had knifed and strangled her, and —

"Oh, Jesus," I said. "The shopping bag lady."
Aaron Creighton nodded.

New York is full of them. East Side, West Side, each neighborhood has its own supply of bag women. Some of them are alcoholic but most of them have gone mad without any help from drink. They walk the streets, huddle on stoops or in doorways. They find sermons in stones and treasures in trash cans. They talk to themselves, to passersby, to God. Sometimes they mumble. Now and then they shriek.

They carry things around with them, the bag women. The shopping bags supply their generic name and their chief common denominator. Most of them seem to be paranoid, and their madness convinces them that their possessions are very valuable, that their enemies covet them. So their shopping bags are never out of their sight.

There used to be a colony of these ladies who lived in Grand Central Station. They would sit up all night in the waiting room, taking turns waddling off to the lavatory from time to time. They rarely talked to each other but some herd instinct made them comfortable with one another. But they were not comfortable enough to trust their precious bags to one another's safekeeping, and each sad crazy lady always toted her shopping bags to and from the ladies' room.

Mary Alice Redfield had been a shopping bag lady. I don't know when she set up shop in the neighborhood. I'd been living in the same hotel ever since I resigned from the NYPD and separated from my wife and sons, and that was getting to be quite a few years now. Had Miss Redfield been on the scene that long ago? I couldn't remember her first appearance. Like so many of the neighborhood fixtures, she had been part of the scenery.

Had her death not been violent and abrupt I might never have noticed she was gone.

I'd never known her name. But she had evidently known mine, and had felt something for me that prompted her to leave money to me. How had she come to have money to leave?

She'd had a business of sorts. She would sit on a wooden soft drink case, surrounded by three or four shopping bags, and she would sell newspapers. There's an all-night newsstand at the corner of Fifty-seventh and Eighth, and she would buy a few dozen papers there, carry them a block west to the corner of Ninth, and set up shop in a doorway. She sold the papers at retail, though I suppose some people tipped her a few cents. I could remember a few occasions when I'd bought a paper and waved away change from a dollar bill. Bread upon the waters, perhaps, if that was what had moved her to leave me the money.

I closed my eyes, brought her image into focus. A thick-set woman, stocky rather than fat. Five-three or -four. Dressed usually in shapeless clothing, colorless gray and black garments, layers of clothing that varied with the season. I remembered that she would sometimes wear a hat, an old straw affair with paper and plastic flowers poked into it. And I remembered her eyes, large guileless blue eyes that were many years younger than the rest of her.

Mary Alice Redfield.

"Family money," Aaron Creighton was saying. "She wasn't wealthy but she had come from a family that was comfortably fixed. A bank in Baltimore handled her funds. That's where she was from originally, Baltimore, though she'd lived in New York for as long as anyone can remember. The bank sent her a check every month. Not very much, a couple of hundred dollars, but she hardly spent anything. She paid her rent — "

"I thought she lived on the street."

"No, she had a furnished room a few doors down the street from where she was killed. She lived in another rooming house on Tenth Avenue before that but moved when the building was sold. That was six or seven years ago and she lived on Fifty-fifth Street from then until her death. Her room cost her eighty dollars a month. She spent a few dollars on food. I don't know what she did with the rest. The only money in her room was a coffee can full of pennies. I've been checking the banks and there's no record of a savings account. I suppose she may have spent it or lost it or given it away. She wasn't very firmly grounded in reality."

"No, I don't suppose she was."

He sipped at his coffee. "She probably belonged in an institution," he said. "At least that's what people would say, but she got along in the outside world, she functioned well enough. I don't know if she kept herself clean and I don't know anything about how her mind worked but I think she must have been happier than she would have been in an institution. Don't you think?"

"Probably."

"Of course she wasn't safe, not as it turned out, but anybody can get killed on the streets of New York." He frowned briefly, caught up in a private thought. Then he said, "She came to our office ten years ago. That was before my time." He told me the name of his firm, a string of Anglo-Saxon surnames. "She wanted to draw a will. The original will was a very simple document leaving everything to her sister. Then over the years she would come in from time to time to add codicils leaving specific sums to various persons. She had made a total of thirty-two bequests by the time she died. One was for twenty dollars — that was to a man named John Johnson whom we haven't been able to locate. The remainder all ranged from five hundred to two thousand dollars." He smiled. "I've been given the task of running down the heirs."

"When did she put me into her will?"

"Two years ago in April."

I tried to think what I might have done for her then, how I might have brushed her life with mine. Nothing.

"Of course the will could be contested, Mr. Scudder. It would be easy to challenge Miss Redfield's competence and any relative could almost certainly get it set aside. But no one wishes to challenge it. The total amount involved is slightly in excess of a quarter of a million dollars — "

"That much."

"Yes. Miss Redfield received substantially less than the income which her holdings drew over the years, so the principal kept growing during her lifetime. Now the specific bequests she made total thirty-eight thousand dollars, give or take a few hundred, and the residue goes to Miss Redfield's sister. The sister — her name is Mrs. Palmer — is a widow with grown children. She's hospitalized with cancer and heart trouble and I believe diabetic complications and she hasn't long to live. Her children would like to see the estate settled before their mother dies, and they have enough local prominence to hurry the will through probate. So I'm authorized to tender checks for the full amount of the specific bequests on the condition that the legatees sign quit-claims acknowledging that this payment discharges in full the estate's indebtedness to them."

There was more legalese of less importance. Then he gave me papers to sign and the whole procedure ended with a check on the table. It was payable to me and in the amount of twelve hundred dollars and no cents.

I told Creighton I'd pay for his coffee.

I had time to buy myself another drink and still get to my bank before the windows closed. I put a little of Mary Alice Redfield's legacy in my savings account, took some in cash, and sent a money order to Anita and my sons. I stopped at my hotel to check for messages. There weren't any. I had a drink at McGovern's and crossed the street to have another at Polly's Cage. It wasn't five o'clock yet but the bar was doing good business already.

It turned into a funny night. I had dinner at the Greek place and read the *Post*, spent a little time at Joey Farrell's on Fifty-eighth Street, then wound up getting to Armstrong's around ten-thirty or thereabouts. I spent part of the evening alone at my usual table and part of it in conversation at the bar. I made a point of stretching my drinks, mixing my bourbon with coffee, making a cup last a while, taking a glass of plain water from time to time.

But that never really works. If you're going to get drunk you'll manage it somehow. The obstacles I placed in my path just kept me up later. By two-thirty I'd done what I had set out to do. I'd made my load and I could go home and sleep it off.

I woke around ten with less of a hangover than I'd earned and no memory of anything after I'd left Armstrong's. I was in my own bed in my own hotel room. And my clothes were hung neatly in the closet, always a good sign on a morning after. So I must have been in fairly good shape. But a certain amount of time was lost to memory, blacked out, gone.

When that first started happening I tended to worry about it. But it's the sort of thing you can get used to.

It was the money, the twelve hundred bucks. I couldn't understand the money. I had done nothing to deserve it. It had been left to me by a poor little rich woman whose name I'd not even known.

It had never occurred to me to refuse the dough. Very early in my career as a cop I'd learned an important precept. When someone put money in your hand you closed your fingers around it and put it in your pocket. I learned that lesson well and never had cause to regret its application. I didn't walk around with my hand out and I never took drug or homicide money but I certainly grabbed all the clean graft that came my way and a certain amount that wouldn't have stood a white glove inspection. If Mary Alice thought I merited twelve hundred dollars, who was I to argue?

Ah, but it didn't quite work that way. Because somehow the money gnawed at me.

After breakfast I went to St. Paul's but there was a service going on, a priest saying Mass, so I didn't stay. I walked down to St. Benedict the Moor's on Fifty-third Street and sat for a few minutes in a pew at the rear. I go to churches to try to think, and I gave it a shot but my mind didn't know where to go.

I slipped six twenties into the poor box. I tithe. It's a habit I got into after I left the department and I still don't know why I do it. God knows. Or maybe He's as mystified as I am. This time, though, there was a certain balance in the act. Mary Alice Redfield had given me twelve hundred dollars for no reason I could comprehend. I was passing on a ten percent commission to the church for no better reason.

I stopped on the way out and lit a couple of candles for various people who weren't alive anymore. One of them was for the bag lady. I didn't see how it could do her any good, but I couldn't imagine how it could harm her, either.

I had read some press coverage of the killing when it happened. I generally keep up with crime stories. Part of me evidently never stopped being a policeman. Now I went down to the Forty-second Street library to refresh my memory.

The *Times* had run a pair of brief back-page items, the first a report of the killing of an unidentified female derelict, the second a follow-up giving her name and age. She'd been forty-seven, I learned. This surprised me, and then I realized that any specific number would have come as a surprise. Bums and bag ladies are ageless. Mary Alice Redfield could have been thirty or sixty or anywhere in between.

The *News* had run a more extended article than the *Times,* enumerating the stab wounds — twenty-six of them — and described the scarf wound about her throat — blue and white, a designer print, but tattered at its edges and evidently somebody's castoff. It was this article that I remembered having read.

But the *Post* had really played the story. It had appeared shortly after the new owner took over the paper and the editors were going all out for human interest, which always translates out as sex and violence. The brutal killing of a woman touches both of those bases, and this had the added kick that she was a character. If they'd ever learned she was an heiress it would have been page three material, but even without that knowledge they did all right by her.

The first story they ran was straight news reporting, albeit embellished with reports on the blood, the clothes she was wearing, the litter in the alley where she was found, and all that sort of thing. The next day a reporter pushed the pathos button and tapped out a story featuring capsule interviews with people in the neighborhood. Only a few of them were identified by name and I came away with the feeling that he'd made up some peachy quotes and attributed them to unnamed nonexistent hangers-on. As a sidebar to that story, another reporter speculated on the possibility of a whole string of bag lady murders, a speculation which happily had turned out to be off the mark. The clown had presumably gone around the West Side asking shopping bag ladies if they were afraid of being the killer's next victim. I hope he faked the piece and let the ladies alone.

And that was about it. When the killer failed to strike again the newspapers hung up on the story. Good news is no news.

I walked back from the library. It was fine weather. The winds had blown all the crap out of the sky and there was nothing but blue overhead. The air actually had some air in it for a change. I walked west on Forty-second Street and north on Broadway, and I started noticing the number of street people, the drunks and the crazies and the unclassifiable derelicts. By the time I got within a few blocks of Fifty-seventh Street I was recognizing a large percentage of them. Each mini-neighborhood has its own human flotsam and jetsam and they're a lot more noticeable come springtime. Winter sends some of them south and others to shelter, and there's a certain percentage who die of exposure, but when the sun warms the pavement it brings most of them out again.

When I stopped for a paper at the corner of Eighth Avenue I got the bag lady into the conversation. The newsie clucked his tongue and shook his head. "The damnedest thing. Just the damnedest thing."

"Murder never makes much sense."

"The hell with murder. You know what she did? You know Eddie, works for me midnight to eight? Guy with the one droopy eyelid? Now he wasn't the guy used to sell her the stack of papers. Matter of fact that was usually me. She'd come by during the late morning or early afternoon and she'd take fifteen or twenty papers and pay me for 'em, and then she'd sit on her crate down the next corner and she'd sell as many as she could, and then she'd bring 'em back and I'd give her a refund on what she didn't sell."

"What did she pay for them?"

"Full price. And that's what she sold 'em for. The hell, I can't discount on papers. You know the margin we got. I'm not even supposed to take 'em back, but what difference does it make? It gave the poor woman something to do is my theory. She was important, she was a businesswoman. Sits there charging a quarter for something she just paid a quarter for, it's no way to get rich, but you know something? She had money. Lived like a pig but she had money."

"So I understand."

"She left Eddie seven-twenty. You believe that? Seven hundred and twenty dollars, she willed it to him, there was this lawyer come around two, three weeks ago with a check. Eddie Halloran. Pay to the order of. You believe that? She never had dealings with him. I sold her the papers, I bought 'em back from her. Not that I'm complaining, not that I want the woman's money, but I ask you this: Why Eddie? He don't know her. He can't believe she knows his name, Eddie Halloran. Why'd she leave it to him? He tells this lawyer, he says maybe she's got some other Eddie Halloran in mind. It's a common Irish name and the neighborhood's full of the Irish. I'm thinking to myself, Eddie, schmuck, take the money and shut up, but it's him all right because it says in the will. Eddie Halloran the newsdealer is what it says. So that's him, right? But why Eddie?"

Why me? "Maybe she liked the way he smiled."

"Yeah, maybe. Or the way he combed his hair. Listen, it's money in his pocket. I worried he'd go on a toot, drink it up, but he says money's no temptation. He says he's always got the price of a drink in his jeans and there's a bar on every block but he can walk right past 'em, so why worry about a few hundred dollars? You know something? That crazy woman, I'll tell you something, I miss her. She'd come, crazy hat on her head, spacy look in her eyes, she'd buy her stack of papers and waddle off all businesslike, then she'd bring the leftovers and cash 'em in, and I'd make a joke about her when she was out of earshot, but I miss her."

"I know what you mean."

"She never hurt nobody," he said. "She never hurt a soul."

"Mary Alice Redfield. Yeah, the multiple stabbing and strangulation." He shifted a cud-sized wad of gum from one side of his mouth to the other, pushed a lock of hair off his forehead, and yawned. "What have you got, some new information?"

"Nothing. I wanted to find out what you had."

"Yeah, right."

He worked on the chewing gum. He was a patrolman named Andersen who worked out of the Eighteenth. Another cop, a detective named Guzik, had learned that Andersen had caught the Redfield case and had taken the trouble to introduce the two of us. I hadn't known Andersen when I was on the force. He was younger than I, but then most people are nowadays.

He said, "Thing is, Scudder, we more or less put that one out of the way. It's in an open file. You know how it works. If we get new information, fine, but in the meantime I don't sit up nights thinking about it."

"I just wanted to see what you had."

"Well, I'm kind of tight for time, if you know what I mean. My own personal time, I set a certain store by my own time."

"I can understand that."

"You probably got some relative of the deceased for a client. Wants to find out who'd do such a terrible thing to poor old Cousin Mary. Naturally you're interested because it's a chance to make a buck and a man's gotta make a living. Whether a man's a cop or a civilian he's gotta make a buck, right?"

Uh-huh. I seem to remember that we were subtler in my day, but perhaps that's just age talking. I thought of telling him that I didn't have a client but why should he believe me? He didn't know me. If there was nothing in it for him, why should he bother?

So I said, "You know, we're just a couple weeks away from Memorial Day."

"Yeah, I'll buy a poppy from a Legionnaire. So what else is new?"

"Memorial Day's when women start wearing white shoes and men put straw hats on their heads. You got a new hat for the summer season, Andersen? Because you could use one."

"A man can always use a new hat," he said.

A hat is cop talk for twenty-five dollars. By the time I left the precinct house Andersen had two tens and a five of Mary Alice Redfield's bequest to me and I had all the data that had turned up to date.

I think Andersen won that one. I now knew that the murder weapon had been a kitchen knife with a blade approximately seven and a half inches long. That one of the stab wounds had found the heart and had probably caused death instantaneously. That it was impossible to determine whether strangulation had taken place before or after death. That should have been possible to determine — maybe the medical examiner hadn't wasted too much time checking her out, or maybe he had been reluctant to commit himself. She'd been dead a few hours when they found her — the estimate was that she'd died around midnight and the body wasn't reported until half-past five. That wouldn't have ripened her all that much, not in winter weather, but most likely her personal hygiene was nothing to boast about, and she was just a shopping bag lady and you couldn't bring her back to life, so why knock yourself out running tests on her malodorous corpse?

I learned a few other things. The landlady's name. The name of the off-duty bartender, heading home after a nightcap at the neighborhood after-hours joint, who'd happened on the body and who had been drunk enough or sober enough to take the trouble to report it. And I learned the sort of negative facts that turn up in a police report when the case is headed for an open file — the handful of non-leads that led nowhere, the witnesses who had nothing to contribute, the routine matters routinely handled. They hadn't knocked themselves out, Andersen and his partner, but would I have handled it any differently? Why knock yourself out chasing a murderer you didn't stand much chance of catching?

In the theater, SRO is good news. It means a sellout performance, standing room only. But once you get out of the theater district it means single room occupancy, and the designation is invariably applied to a hotel or apartment house which has seen better days.

Mary Alice Redfield's home for the last six or seven years of her life had started out as an old Rent Law tenement, built around the turn of the century, six stories tall, faced in red-brown brick, with four apartments to the floor. Now all of those little apartments had been carved into single rooms as if they were election districts gerrymandered by a maniac. There was a communal bathroom on each floor and you didn't need a map to find it.

The manager was a Mrs. Larkin. Her blue eyes had lost most of their color and half her hair had gone from black to gray but she was still pert. If she's reincarnated as a bird she'll be a house wren.

She said, "Oh, poor Mary. We're none of us safe, are we, with the streets full of monsters? I was born in this neighborhood and I'll die in it, but please God that'll be of natural causes. Poor Mary. There's some said she should have been locked up, but Jesus, she got along. She lived her life. And she had her check coming in every month and paid her rent on time. She had her own money, you know. She wasn't living off the public like some I could name but won't."

"I know."

"Do you want to see her room? I rented it twice since then. The first one was a young man and he didn't stay. He looked all right but when he left me I was just as glad. He said he was a sailor off a ship and when he left he said he'd got on with another ship and was on his way to Hong Kong or some such place, but I've had no end of sailors and he didn't walk like a sailor so I don't know what he was after doing. Then I could have rented it twelve times but didn't because I won't rent to colored or Spanish. I've nothing against them but I won't have them in the house. The owner says to me, Mrs. Larkin he says, my instructions are to rent to anybody regardless of race or creed or color, but if you was to use your own judgment I wouldn't have to know about it. In other words he don't want them either but he's after covering himself."

"I suppose he has to."

"Oh, with all the laws, but I've had no trouble." She laid a forefinger alongside her nose. It's a gesture you don't see too much these days. "Then I rented poor Mary's room two weeks ago to a very nice woman, a widow. She likes her beer, she does, but why shouldn't she have it? I keep my eye on her and she's making no trouble, and if she wants an old jar now and then whose business is it but her own?" She fixed her blue-gray eyes on me. "You like your drink," she said.

"Is it on my breath?"

"No, but I can see it in your face. Larkin liked his drink and there's some say it killed him but he liked it and a man has a right to live what life he wants. And he was never a hard man when he drank, never cursed or fought or beat a woman as some I could name but won't. Mrs. Shepard's out now. That's the one took poor Mary's room, and I'll show it to you if you want."

So I saw the room. It was kept neat.

"She keeps it tidier than poor Mary," Mrs. Larkin said. "Now Mary wasn't dirty, you understand, but she had all her belongings. Her shopping bags and other things that she kept in her room. She made a mare's nest of the place, and all the years she lived here, you see, it wasn't tidy. I would keep her bed made but she didn't want me touching her things and so I let it be cluttered as she wanted it. She paid her rent on time and made no trouble otherwise. She had money, you know."

"Yes, I know."

"She left some to a woman on the fourth floor. A much younger woman, she'd only moved here three months before Mary was killed, and if she exchanged a word with Mary I couldn't swear to it, but Mary left her almost a thousand dollars. Now Mrs. Klein across the hall lived here since before Mary ever moved in and the two old things always had a good word for each other, and all Mrs. Klein has is the welfare and she could have made good use of a couple of dollars, but Mary left her money instead to Miss Strom." She raised her eyebrows to show bewilderment. "Now Mrs. Klein said nothing, and I don't even know if she's had the thought that Mary might have mentioned her in her will, but Miss Strom said she didn't know what to make of it. She just couldn't understand it at all, and what I told her was you can't figure out a woman like poor Mary who never had both her feet on the pavement. Troubled as she was, daft as she was, who's to say what she might have had on her mind?"

"Could I see Miss Strom?"

"That would be for her to say, but she's not home from work yet. She works part-time in the afternoons. She's a close one, not that she hasn't the right to be, and she's never said what it is that she does. But she's a decent sort. This is a decent house."

"I'm sure it is."

"It's single rooms and they don't cost much so you know you're not at the Ritz Hotel, but there's decent people here and I keep it as clean as a person can. When there's not but one toilet on the floor it's a struggle. But it's decent."

"Yes."

"Poor Mary. Why'd anyone kill her? Was it sex, do you know? Not that you could imagine anyone wanting her, the old thing, but try to figure out a madman and you'll go mad your own self. Was she molested?"

"No."

"Just killed, then. Oh, God save us all. I gave her a home for almost seven years. Which it was no more than my job to do, not making it out to be charity on my part. But I had her here all that time and of course I never knew her, you couldn't get to know a poor old soul like that, but I got used to her. Do you know what I mean?"

"I think so."

"I got used to having her about. I might say Hello and Good morning and Isn't it a nice day and not get a look in reply, but even on those days she was someone familiar to say something to. And she's gone now and we're all of us older, aren't we?"

"We are."

"The poor old thing. How could anyone do it, will you tell me that? How could anyone murder her?"

I don't think she expected an answer. Just as well. I didn't have one.

After dinner I returned for a few minutes of conversation with Genevieve Strom. She had no idea why Miss Redfield had left her the money. She'd received $880 and she was glad to get it because she could use it, but the whole thing puzzled her. "I hardly knew her," she said more than once. "I keep thinking I ought to do something special with the money, but what?"

I made the bars that night but drinking didn't

have the urgency it had possessed the night before. I was able to keep it in proportion and to know that I'd wake up the next morning with my memory intact. In the course of things I dropped over to the newsstand a little past midnight and talked with Eddie Halloran. He was looking good and I said as much. I remembered him when he'd gone to work for Sid three years ago. He'd been drawn then, and shaky, and his eyes always moved off to the side of whatever he was looking at. Now there was confidence in his stance and he looked years younger. It hadn't all come back to him and maybe some of it was lost forever. I guess the booze had him pretty good before he kicked it once and for all.

We talked about the bag lady. He said, "Know what I think it is? Somebody's sweeping the streets."

"I don't follow you."

"A cleanup campaign. Few years back, Matt, there was this gang of kids found a new way to amuse theirselves. Pick up a can of gasoline, find some bum down on the Bowery, pour the gas on him, and throw a lit match at him. You remember?"

"Yeah, I remember."

"Those kids thought they were patriots. Thought they deserved a medal. They were cleaning up the neighborhood, getting drunken bums off the streets. You know, Matt, people don't like to look at a derelict. That building up the block, the Towers? There's this grating there where the heating system's vented. You remember how the guys would sleep there in the winter. It was warm, it was comfortable, it was free, and two or three guys would be there every night catching some Z's and getting warm. Remember?"

"Uh-huh. Then they fenced it."

"Right. Because the tenants complained. It didn't hurt them any, it was just the local bums sleeping it off, but the tenants pay a lot of rent and they don't like to look at bums on their way in or out of their building. The bums were outside and not bothering anybody but it was the sight of them, you know, so the owners went to the expense of putting up cyclone fencing around where they used to sleep. It looks ugly as hell and all it does is keep the bums out but that's all it's supposed to do."

"That's human beings for you."

He nodded, then turned aside to sell somebody a *Daily News* and a *Racing Form*. Then he said, "I don't know what it is exactly. I was a bum, Matt. I got pretty far down. You probably don't know how far. I got as far as the Bowery. I panhandled, I slept in my clothes on a bench or in a doorway. You look at men like that and you think they're just waiting to die, and they are, but some of them come back. And you can't tell for sure who's gonna come back and who's not. Somebody coulda poured gas on me, set me on fire. Sweet Jesus."

"The shopping bag lady — "

"You'll look at a bum and you'll say to yourself, 'Maybe I could get like that and I don't wanta think about it.' Or you'll look at somebody like the shopping bag lady and say, 'I could go nutsy like her so get her out of my sight.' And you get people who think like Nazis. You know, take all the cripples and the lunatics and the retarded kids and all and give 'em an injection and Good-bye, Charlie."

"You think that's what happened to her?"

"What else?"

"But whoever did it stopped at one, Eddie."

He frowned. "Don't make sense," he said. "Unless he did the one job and the next day he got run down by a Ninth Avenue bus, and it couldn't happen to a nicer guy. Or he got scared. All that blood and it was more than he figured on. Or he left town. Could be anything like that."

"Could be."

"There's no other reason, is there? She musta been killed because she was a bag lady, right?"

"I don't know."

"Well, Jesus Christ, Matt. What other reason would anybody have for killing her?"

The law firm where Aaron Creighton worked had offices on the seventh floor of the Flatiron Building. In addition to the four partners, eleven other lawyers had their names painted on the frosted glass door. Aaron Creighton's came second from the bottom. Well, he was young.

He was also surprised to see me, and when I told him what I wanted he said it was irregular.

"Matter of public record, isn't it?"

"Well, yes," he said. "That means you can find the information. It doesn't mean we're obliged to furnish it to you."

For an instant I thought I was back at the Eighteenth Precinct and a cop was trying to hustle me for the price of a new hat. But Creighton's reservations were ethical. I wanted a list of Mary Alice Redfield's beneficiaries, including the amounts they'd received and the dates they'd been added to her will. He wasn't sure where his duty lay.

"I'd like to be helpful," he said. "Perhaps you could tell me just what your interest is."

"I'm not sure."

"I beg your pardon?"

"I don't know why I'm playing with this one. I used to be a cop, Mr. Creighton. Now I'm a sort of unofficial detective. I don't carry a license but I do things for people and I wind up making enough that way to keep a roof overhead."

His eyes were wary. I guess he was trying to guess how I intended to earn myself a fee out of this.

"I got twelve hundred dollars out of the blue. It was left to me by a woman I didn't really know and who didn't really know me. I can't seem to slough off the feeling that I got the money for a reason. That I've been paid in advance."

"Paid for what?"

"To try and find out who killed her."

"Oh," he said. "*Oh.*"

"I don't want to get the heirs together to challenge the will, if that was what was bothering you. And I can't quite make myself suspect that one of her beneficiaries killed her for the money she was leaving him. For one thing, she doesn't seem to have told people they were named in her will. She never said anything to me or to the two people I've spoken with thus far. For another, it wasn't the sort of murder that gets committed for gain. It was deliberately brutal."

"Then why do you want to know who the other beneficiaries are?"

"I don't know. Part of it's cop training. When you've got any specific leads, any hard facts, you run them down before you cast a wider net. That's only part of it. I suppose I want to get more of a sense of the woman. That's probably all I can realistically hope to get, anyway. I don't stand much chance of tracking her killer."

"The police don't seem to have gotten very far."

I nodded. "I don't think they tried too hard. And I don't think they knew she had an estate. I talked to one of the cops on the case and if he had known that he'd have mentioned it to me. There was nothing in her file. My guess is they waited for her killer to run a string of murders so they'd have something more concrete to work with. It's the kind of senseless crime that usually gets repeated." I closed my eyes for a moment, reaching for an errant thought. "But he didn't repeat," I said. "So they put it on a back burner and then they took it off the stove altogether."

"I don't know much about police work. I'm involved largely with estates and trusts." He tried a smile. "Most of my clients die of natural causes. Murder's an exception. "

"It generally is. I'll probably never find him. I certainly don't expect to find him. Just killing her and moving on, hell, and it was all those months ago. He could have been a sailor off a ship, got tanked up and went nuts and he's in Macao or Port-au-Prince by now. No witnesses and no clues and no suspects and the trail's three months cold by now, and it's a fair bet the killer doesn't remember what he did. So many murders take place in blackout, you know."

"Blackout?" He frowned. "You don't mean in the dark?"

"Alcoholic blackout. The prisons are full of men who got drunk and shot their wives or their best friends. Now they're serving twenty-to-life for something they don't remember. No recollection at all."

The idea unsettled him, and he looked especially young now. "That's frightening," he said. "Really terrifying."

"Yes."

"I originally gave some thought to criminal law. My Uncle Jack talked me out of it. He said you either starve or you spend your time helping professional criminals beat the system. He said that was the only way you made good money out of a criminal practice and what you wound up doing was unpleasant and basically immoral. Of course there are a couple of superstar criminal lawyers, the hotshots everybody knows, but the other ninety-nine percent fit what Uncle Jack said."

"I would think so, yes."

"I guess I made the right decision." He took his glasses off, inspected them, decided they were clean, put them back on again. "Sometimes I'm not so sure," he said. "Sometimes I wonder. I'll get that list for you. I should probably check with someone to make sure it's all right but I'm not going to bother. You know lawyers. If you ask them whether it's all right to do something they'll automatically say no. Because inaction is always safer than action and they can't get in trouble for giving you bad advice if they tell you to sit on your hands and do nothing. I'm going overboard. Most of the time I like what I do and I'm proud of my profession. This'll take me a few minutes. Do you want some coffee in the meantime?"

His girl brought me a cup, black, no sugar. No bourbon, either. By the time I was done with the coffee he had the list ready.

"If there's anything else I can do — "

I told him I'd let him know. He walked out to the elevator with me, waited for the cage to come wheezing up, shook my hand. I watched him turn and head back to his office and I had the feeling he'd have preferred to come along with me. In a day or so he'd change his mind, but right now he didn't seem too crazy about his job.

The next week was a curious one. I worked my way through the list Aaron Creighton had given me, knowing what I was doing was essentially purposeless but compulsive about doing it all the same.

There were thirty-two names on the list. I checked off my own and Eddie Halloran and Genevieve Strom. I put additional check marks next to six people who lived outside of New York. Then I had a go at the remaining twenty-three names. Creighton had done most of the spadework for me, finding addresses to match most of the names. He'd included the date each of the thirty-two codicils had been drawn, and that enabled me to attack the list in reverse chronological order, starting with those persons who'd been made beneficiaries most recently. If this was a method, there was madness to it; it was based on the notion that a person added recently to the will would be more likely to commit homicide for gain, and I'd already decided this wasn't that kind of a killing to begin with.

Well, it gave me something to do. And it led to some interesting conversations. If the people Mary Alice Redfield had chosen to remember ran to any type, my mind wasn't subtle enough to discern it. They ranged in age, in ethnic background, in gender and sexual orientation, in economic status. Most of them were as mystified as Eddie and Genevieve and I about the bag lady's largesse, but once in a while I'd encounter someone who attributed it to some act of kindness he'd performed, and there was a young man named Jerry Forgash who was in no doubt whatsoever. He was some form of Jesus freak and he'd given poor Mary a couple of tracts and a Get Smart — Get Saved button, presumably a twin to the one he wore on the breast pocket of his chambray shirt. I suppose she put his gifts in one of her shopping bags.

"I told her Jesus loved her," he said, "and I suppose it won her soul for Christ. So of course she was grateful. Cast your bread upon the waters, Mr. Scudder. Brother Matthew. You know there was a disciple of Christ named Matthew."

"I know."

He told me Jesus loved me and that I should get smart and get saved. I managed not to get a button but I had to take a couple of tracts from him. I didn't have a shopping bag so I stuck them in my pocket, and a couple of nights later I read them before I went to bed. They didn't win my soul for Christ but you never know.

I didn't run the whole list. People were hard to find and I wasn't in any big rush to find them. It wasn't that kind of a case. It wasn't a case at all, really, merely an obsession, and there was surely no need to race the clock. Or the calendar. If anything, I was probably reluctant to finish up the names on the list. Once I ran out of them I'd have to find some other way to approach the woman's murder and I was damned if I knew where to start.

While I was doing all this, an odd thing happened. The word got around that I was investigating the woman's death, and the whole neighborhood became very much aware of Mary Alice Redfield. People began to seek me out. Ostensibly they had information to give me or theories to advance, but neither the information nor the theories ever seemed to amount to anything substantial, and I came to see that they were merely there as a prelude to conversation. Someone would start off by saying he'd seen Mary selling the *Post* the afternoon before she was killed, and that would serve as the opening wedge of a discussion of the bag woman, or bag women in general, or various qualities of the neighborhood, or violence in American life, or whatever.

A lot of people started off talking about the bag lady and wound up talking about themselves. I guess most conversations work out that way.

A nurse from Roosevelt said she never saw a shopping bag lady without hearing an inner voice say *There but for the grace of God.* And she was not the only woman who confessed she worried about ending up that way. I guess it's a specter that haunts women who live alone, just as the vision of the Bowery derelict clouds the peripheral vision of hard-drinking men.

Genevieve Strom turned up at Armstrong's one night. We talked briefly about the bag lady. Two nights later she came back again and we took turns spending our inheritances on rounds of drinks. The drinks hit her with some force and a little past midnight she decided it was time to go. I said I'd see her home. At the corner of Fifty-seventh Street she stopped in her tracks and said, "No men in the room. That's one of Mrs. Larkin's rules."

"Old-fashioned, isn't she?"

"She runs a daycent establishment." Her mock-Irish accent was heavier than the landlady's. Her eyes, hard to read in the lamplight, raised to meet mine. "Take me someplace."

I took her to my hotel, a less decent establishment than Mrs. Larkin's. We did each other little good but no harm, and it beat being alone.

Another night I ran into Barry Mosedale at Polly's Cage. He told me there was a singer at Kid Gloves who was doing a number about the bag lady. "I can find out how you can reach him," he offered.

"Is he there now?"

He nodded and checked his watch. "He goes on in fifteen minutes. But you don't want to go there, do you?"

"Why not?"

"Hardly your sort of crowd, Matt."

"Cops go anywhere."

"Indeed they do, and they're welcome wherever they go, aren't they? Just let me drink this and I'll accompany you, if that's all right. You need someone to lend you immoral support."

Kid Gloves is a gay bar on Fifty-sixth west of Ninth. The decor is just a little aggressively gay lib. There's a small raised stage, a scattering of tables, a piano, a loud jukebox. Barry Mosedale and I stood at the bar. I'd been there before and knew better than to order their coffee. I had straight bourbon. Barry had his on ice with a splash of soda.

Halfway through the drink Gordon Lurie was introduced. He wore tight jeans and a flowered shirt, sat on stage on a folding chair, sang ballads he'd written himself with his own guitar for accompaniment. I don't know if he was any good or not. It sounded to me as though all the songs had the same melody, but that may just have been a similarity of style. I don't have much of an ear.

After a song about a summer romance in Amsterdam, Gordon Lurie announced that the next number was dedicated to the memory of Mary Alice Redfield. Then he sang:

*"She's a shopping bag lady who lives on
the sidewalks of Broadway
Wearing all of her clothes and her years
on her back
Toting dead dreams in an old paper sack
Searching the trash cans for something
she lost here on Broadway —
Shopping bag lady . . .*

*"You'd never know but she once was an
actress on Broadway
Speaking the words that they stuffed in
her head*

Reciting the lines of the life that she led
Thrilling her fans and her friends and her
lovers on Broadway —
Shopping bag lady . . .

"There are demons who lurk in the corners
of minds and of Broadway
And after the omens and portents and
signs
Came the day she forgot to remember her
lines
Put her life on a leash and took it out
walking on Broadway —
Shopping bag lady . . ."

There were a couple more verses and the shopping bag lady in the song wound up murdered in a doorway, dying in defense of the "tattered old treasures she mined in the trash cans of Broadway." The song went over well and got a bigger hand than any of the ones that had preceded it.

I asked Barry who Gordon Lurie was.

"You know very nearly as much as I," he said. "He started here Tuesday. I find him whelming, personally. Neither overwhelming nor underwhelming but somewhere in the middle."

"Mary Alice never spent much time on Broadway. I never saw her more than a block from Ninth Avenue."

"Poetic license, I'm sure. The song would lack a certain something if you substituted Ninth Avenue for Broadway. As it stands it sounds a little like 'Rhinestone Cowboy.'"

"Lurie live around here?"

"I don't know where he lives. I have the feeling he's Canadian. So many people are nowadays. It used to be that no one was Canadian and now simply everybody is. I'm sure it must be a virus."

We listened to the rest of Gordon Lurie's act. Then Barry leaned forward and chatted with the bartender to find out how I could get backstage. I found my way to what passed for a dressing room at Kid Gloves. It must have been a ladies' lavatory in a prior incarnation.

I went in there thinking I'd made a breakthrough, that Lurie had killed her and now he was dealing with his guilt by singing about her. I don't think I really believed this but it supplied me with direction and momentum.

I told him my name and that I was interested in his act. He wanted to know if I was from a record company. "Am I on the threshold of a great opportunity? Am I about to become an overnight success after years of travail?"

We got out of the tiny room and left the club through a side door. Three doors down the block we sat in a cramped booth at a coffee shop. He ordered a Greek salad and we both had coffee.

I told him I was interested in his song about the bag lady.

He brightened. "Oh, do you like it? Personally I think it's the best thing I've written. I just wrote it a couple of days ago. I opened next door Tuesday night. I got to New York three weeks ago and I had a two-week booking in the West Village. A place called David's Table. Do you know it?"

"I don't think so."

"Another stop on the K-Y circuit. Either there aren't any straight people in New York or they don't go to nightclubs. But I was there two weeks, and then I opened at Kid Gloves, and afterward I was sitting and drinking with some people and somebody was talking about the shopping bag lady and I had had enough Amaretto to be maudlin on the subject. I woke up Wednesday morning with a splitting headache and the first verse of the song buzzing in my splitting head, and I sat up immediately and wrote it down, and as I was writing one verse the next would come bubbling to the surface, and before I knew it I had all six verses." He took a cigarette, then paused in the act of lighting it to fix his eyes on me. "You told me your name," he said, "but I don't remember it."

"Matthew Scudder."

"Yes. You're the person investigating her murder."

"I'm not sure that's the right word. I've been talking to people, seeing what I can come up with. Did you know her before she was killed?"

He shook his head. "I was never even in this neighborhood before. *Oh.* I'm not a suspect, am I? Because I haven't been in New York since the fall. I haven't bothered to figure out where I was when she was killed but I was in California at Christmastime and I'd gotten as far east as Chicago in early March, so I do have a fairly solid alibi."

"I never really suspected you. I think I just wanted to hear your song." I sipped some coffee. "Where did you get the facts of her life? Was she an actress?"

"I don't think so. Was she? It wasn't really *about* her, you know. It was inspired by her story but I didn't know her and I never knew anything about her. The past few days I've been paying a lot of attention to bag ladies, though. And other street people."

"I know what you mean."

"Are there more of them in New York or is it just that they're so much more visible here? In California everybody drives, you don't see people on the street. I'm from Canada, rural Ontario, and the first city I ever spent much time in was Toronto, and there are crazy people on the streets there but it's nothing like New

York. Does the city drive them crazy or does it just tend to draw crazy people?"

"I don't know."

"Maybe they're not crazy. Maybe they just hear a different drummer. I wonder who killed her."

"We'll probably never know."

"What I really wonder is *why* she was killed. In my song I made up some reason. That somebody wanted what was in her bags. I think it works as a song that way but I don't think there's much chance that it happened like that. Why would anyone kill the poor thing?"

"I don't know."

"They say she left people money. People she hardly knew. Is that the truth?" I nodded. "And she left me a song. I don't even feel that I wrote it. I woke up with it. I never set eyes on her and she touched my life. That's strange, isn't it?"

Everything was strange. The strangest part of all was the way it ended.

It was a Monday night. The Mets were at Shea and I'd taken my sons to a game. The Dodgers were in for a three-game series which they eventually swept as they'd been sweeping everything lately. The boys and I got to watch them knock Jon Matlack out of the box and go on to shell his several replacements. The final count was something like 13 – 4. We stayed in our seats until the last out. Then I saw them home and caught a train back to the city.

So it was past midnight when I reached Armstrong's. Trina brought me a large double and a mug of coffee without being asked. I knocked back half of the bourbon and was dumping the rest into my coffee when she told me somebody'd been looking for me earlier. "He was in three times in the past two hours," she said. "A wiry guy, high forehead, bushy eyebrows, sort of a bulldog jaw. I guess the word for it is underslung."

"Perfectly good word."

"I said you'd probably get here sooner or later."

"I always do. Sooner or later."

"Uh-huh. You okay, Matt?"

"The Mets lost a close one."

"I heard it was thirteen to four."

"That's close for them these days. Did he say what it was about?"

He hadn't, but within the half hour he came in again and I was there to be found. I recognized him from Trina's description as soon as he came through the door. He looked faintly familiar but he was nobody I knew. I suppose I'd seen him around the neighborhood.

Evidently he knew me by sight because he found his way to my table without asking directions and took a chair without being invited to sit. He didn't say anything for a while and neither did I. I had a fresh bourbon and coffee in front of me and I took a sip and looked him over.

He was under thirty. His cheeks were hollow and the flesh of his face was stretched over his skull like leather that had shrunk upon drying. He wore a forest green work shirt and a pair of khaki pants. He needed a shave.

Finally he pointed at my cup and asked me what I was drinking. When I told him he said all he drank was beer.

"They have beer here," I said.

"Maybe I'll have what you're drinking." He turned in his chair and waved for Trina. When she came over he said he'd have bourbon and coffee, the same as I was having. He didn't say anything more until she brought the drink. Then, after he had spent quite some time stirring it, he took a sip. "Well," he said, "that's not so bad. That's okay."

"Glad you like it."

"I don't know if I'd order it again, but at least now I know what it's like."

"That's something."

"I seen you around. Matt Scudder. Used to be a cop, private eye now, blah blah blah. Right?"

"Close enough."

"My name's Floyd. I never liked it but I'm stuck with it, right? I could change but who'm I kidding? Right?"

"If you say so."

"If I don't somebody else will. Floyd Karp, that's the full name. I didn't tell you my last name, did I? That's it, Floyd Karp."

"Okay."

"Okay, okay, okay." He pursed his lips, blew out air in a silent whistle. "What do we do now, Matt? Huh? That's what I want to know."

"I'm not sure what you mean, Floyd."

"Oh, you know what I'm getting at, driving at, getting at. You know, don't you?"

By this time I suppose I did.

"I killed that old lady. Took her life, stabbed her with my knife." He flashed the saddest smile. "Steee-rangled her with her skeeee-arf. Hoist her with her own whatchacallit, petard. What's a petard, Matt?"

"I don't know, Floyd. Why'd you kill her?"

He looked at me, he looked at his coffee, he looked at me again.

He said, "Had to."

"Why?"

"Same as the bourbon and coffee. Had to *see*. Had to taste it and find out what it was like." His eyes met mine. His were very large, hollow, empty. I fancied I could see right through them to the blackness at the back of his skull. "I couldn't get my mind away from murder," he said. His voice was more sober now, the mocking playful quality gone from it. "I tried. I just couldn't do it. It was on my mind all the time and I was afraid of what I might do. I couldn't function, I couldn't think, I just saw blood and death all the time. I was afraid to close my eyes for fear of what I might see. I would just stay up, days it seemed, and then I'd be tired enough to pass out the minute I closed my eyes. I stopped eating. I used to be fairly heavy and the weight just fell off of me."

"When did all this happen, Floyd?"

"I don't know. All winter. And I thought if I went and did it once I would know if I was a man or a monster or what. And I got this knife, and I went out a couple nights but lost my nerve, and then one night — I don't want to talk about that part of it now."

"All right."

"I almost couldn't do it, but I couldn't not do it, and then I was doing it and it went on forever. It was *horrible*."

"Why didn't you stop?"

"I don't know. I think I was afraid to stop. That doesn't make any sense, does it? I just don't know. It was all crazy, insane, like being in a movie and being in the audience at the same time. Watching myself."

"No one saw you do it?"

"No. I threw the knife down a sewer. I went home. I put all my clothes in the incinerator, the ones I was wearing. I kept throwing up. All that night I would throw up even when my stomach was empty. Dry heaves, Department of Dry Heaves. And then I guess I fell asleep, I don't know when or how but I did, and the next day I woke up and thought I dreamed it. But of course I didn't."

"No."

"And what I did think was that it was over. I did it

and I knew I'd never want to do it again. It was something crazy that happened and I could forget about it. And I thought that was what happened."

"That you managed to forget about it?"

A nod. "But I guess I didn't. And now everybody's talking about her. Mary Alice Redfield, I killed her without knowing her name. Nobody knew her name and now everybody knows it and it's all back in my mind. And I heard you were looking for me, and I guess, I guess . . ." He frowned, chasing a thought around in his mind like a dog trying to capture his tail. Then he gave it up and looked at me. "So here I am," he said. "So here I am."

"Yes."

"Now what happens?"

"I think you'd better tell the police about it, Floyd."

"Why?"

"I suppose for the same reason you told me."

He thought about it. After a long time he nodded. "All right," he said. "I can accept that. I'd never kill anybody again. I know that. But — you're right. I have to tell them. I don't know who to see or what to say or, hell, I just — "

"I'll go with you if you want."

"Yeah. I want you to."

"I'll have a drink and then we'll go. You want another?"

"No. I'm not much of a drinker."

I had it without the coffee this time. After Trina brought it I asked him how he'd picked his victim. Why the bag lady?

He started to cry. No sobs, just tears spilling from his deep-set eyes. After a while he wiped them on his sleeve.

"Because she didn't count," he said. "That's what I thought. She was nobody. Who cared if she died? Who'd miss her?" He closed his eyes tight. "Everybody misses her," he said. "Everybody."

So I took him in. I don't know what they'll do with him. It's not my problem.

It wasn't really a case and I didn't really solve it. As far as I can see I didn't do anything. It was the talk that drove Floyd Karp from cover, and no doubt I helped some of the talk get started, but some of it would have gotten around without me. All those legacies of Mary Alice Redfield's had made her a nine-day wonder in the neighborhood. It was one of those legacies that got me involved.

Maybe she caught her own killer. Maybe he caught himself, as everyone does. Maybe no man's an island and maybe everybody is.

All I know is I lit a candle for the woman, and I suspect I'm not the only one who did.

BY THE DAWN'S EARLY LIGHT

All this happened a long time ago.

Abe Beame was living in Gracie Mansion, though even he seemed to have trouble believing he was really the mayor of the city of New York. Ali was in his prime, and the Knicks still had a year or so left in Bradley and DeBusschere. I was still drinking in those days, of course, and at the time it seemed to be doing more for me than it was doing to me.

I had already left my wife and kids, my home in Syosset, and the NYPD. I was living in the hotel on West Fifty-seventh Street where I still live, and I was doing most of my drinking around the corner in Jimmy Armstrong's saloon. Billie was the nighttime bartender. A Filipino youth named Dennis was behind the stick most days.

And Tommy Tillary was one of the regulars.

He was big, probably 6'2", full in the chest, big in the belly, too. He rarely showed up in a suit but always wore a jacket and tie, usually a navy or burgundy blazer with gray-flannel slacks or white duck pants in warmer weather. He had a loud voice that boomed from his barrel chest, and a big, clean-shaven face that was innocent around the pouting mouth and knowing around the eyes. He was somewhere in his late forties and he drank a lot of top-shelf scotch. Chivas, as I remember it, but it could have been Johnnie Black. Whatever it was, his face was beginning to show it, with patches of permanent flush at the cheekbones and a tracery of broken capillaries across the bridge of the nose.

We were saloon friends. We didn't speak every time we ran into each other, but at the least we always acknowledged each other with a nod or a wave. He told a lot of dialect jokes and told them reasonably well, and I laughed at my share of them. Sometimes I was in a mood to reminisce about my days on the force, and when my stories were funny, his laugh was as loud as anyone's.

Sometimes he showed up alone, sometimes with male friends. About a third of the time, he was in the company of a short and curvy blonde named Carolyn. "Carolyn from the Caro-line" was the way he occasionally introduced her, and she did have a faint Southern accent that became more pronounced as the drink got to her.

Then, one morning, I picked up the *Daily News* and read that burglars had broken into a house on Colonial Road, in the Bay Ridge section of Brooklyn. They had stabbed to death the only occupant present, one Margaret Tillary. Her husband, Thomas J. Tillary, a salesman, was not at home at the time.

I hadn't known Tommy was a salesman or that he'd had a wife. He did wear a wide yellow-gold band on the appropriate finger, and it was clear that he wasn't married to Carolyn from the Caroline, and it now looked as though he was a widower. I felt vaguely sorry for him, vaguely sorry for the wife I'd never even known of, but that was the extent of it. I drank enough back then to avoid feeling any emotion very strongly.

And then, two or three nights later, I walked into Armstrong's and there was Carolyn. She didn't appear to be waiting for him or anyone else, nor did she look as though she'd just breezed in a few minutes ago. She had a stool by herself at the bar and she was drinking something dark from a lowball glass.

I took a seat a few stools down from her. I ordered two double shots of bourbon, drank one, and poured the other into the black coffee Billie brought me. I was sipping the coffee when a voice with a Piedmont softness said, "I forget your name."

I looked up.

"I believe we were introduced," she said, "but I don't recall your name."

"It's Matt," I said, "and you're right, Tommy introduced us. You're Carolyn."

"Carolyn Cheatham. Have you seen him?"

"Tommy? Not since it happened."

"Neither have I. Were you-all at the funeral?"

"No. When was it?"

"This afternoon. Neither was I. There. Whyn't you come sit next to me so's I don't have to shout. Please?"

She was drinking a sweet almond liqueur that she took on the rocks. It tastes like dessert, but it's as strong as whiskey.

"He told me not to come," she said. "To the funeral. He said it was a matter of respect for the dead." She picked up her glass and stared into it. I've never known what people hope to see there, though it's a gesture I've performed often enough myself.

"Respect," she said. "What's he care about respect? I would have just been part of the office crowd; we both work at Tannahill; far as anyone there knows, we're just friends. And all we ever were is friends, you know."

"Whatever you say."

"Oh, *shit*," she said. "I don't mean I wasn't fucking

him, for the Lord's sake. I mean it was just laughs and good times. He was married and he went home to Mama every night and that was jes' fine, because who in her right mind'd want Tommy Tillary around by the dawn's early light? Christ in the foothills, did I spill this or drink it?"

We agreed she was drinking them a little too fast. It was this fancy New York sweet-drink shit, she maintained, not like the bourbon she'd grown up on. You knew where you stood with bourbon.

I told her I was a bourbon drinker myself, and it pleased her to learn this. Alliances have been forged on thinner bonds than that, and ours served to propel us out of Armstrong's, with a stop down the block for a fifth of Maker's Mark — her choice — and a four-block walk to her apartment. There were exposed brick walls, I remember, and candles stuck in straw-wrapped bottles, and several travel posters from Sabena, the Belgian airline.

We did what grown-ups do when they find themselves alone together. We drank our fair share of the Maker's Mark and went to bed. She made a lot of enthusiastic noises and more than a few skillful moves, and afterward she cried some.

A little later, she dropped off to sleep. I was tired myself, but I put on my clothes and sent myself home. Because who in her right mind'd want Matt Scudder around by the dawn's early light?

Over the next couple of days, I wondered every time I entered Armstrong's if I'd run into her, and each time I was more relieved than disappointed when I didn't. I didn't encounter Tommy, either, and that, too, was a relief and in no sense disappointing.

Then, one morning, I picked up the *News* and read that they'd arrested a pair of young Hispanics from Sunset Park for the Tillary burglary and homicide. The paper ran the usual photo — two skinny kids, their hair unruly, one of them trying to hide his face from the camera, the other smirking defiantly, and each of them handcuffed to a broad-shouldered, grim-faced Irishman in a suit. You didn't need the careful caption to tell the good guys from the bad guys.

Sometime in the middle of the afternoon, I went over to Armstrong's for a hamburger and drank a beer with it. The phone behind the bar rang and Dennis put down the glass he was wiping and answered it. "He was here a minute ago," he said. "I'll see if he stepped out." He covered the mouthpiece with his hand and looked quizzically at me. "Are you still here?" he asked. "Or did you slip away while my attention was diverted?"

"Who wants to know?"

"Tommy Tillary."

You never know what a woman will decide to tell a man or how a man will react to it. I didn't want to find out, but I was better off learning over the phone than face-to-face. I nodded and took the phone from Dennis.

I said, "Matt Scudder, Tommy. I was sorry to hear about your wife."

"Thanks, Matt, Jesus, it feels like it happened a year ago. It was what, a week?"

"At least they got the bastards."

There was a pause. Then he said, "Jesus. You haven't seen a paper, huh?"

"That's where I read about it. Two Spanish kids."

"You didn't happen to see this afternoon's *Post*."

"No. Why, what happened? They turn out to be clean?"

"The two spics. Clean? Shit, they're about as clean

as the men's room in the Times Square subway station. The cops hit their place and found stuff from my house everywhere they looked. Jewelry they had descriptions of, a stereo that I gave them the serial number, everything. Monogrammed shit. I mean, that's how clean they were, for Christ's sake."

"So?"

"They admitted the burglary but not the murder."

"That's common, Tommy."

"Lemme finish, huh? They admitted the burglary, but according to them it was a put-up job. According to them, I hired them to hit my place. They could keep whatever they got and I'd have everything out and arranged for them, and in return I got to clean up on the insurance by overreporting the loss."

"What did the loss amount to?"

"Shit, *I* don't know. There were twice as many things turned up in their apartment as I ever listed when I made out a report. There's things I missed a few days after I filed the report and others I didn't know were gone until the cops found them. You don't notice everything right away, at least I didn't, and on top of it, how could I think straight with Peg dead? You know?"

"It hardly sounds like an insurance setup."

"No, of course it wasn't. How the hell could it be? All I had was a standard homeowner's policy. It covered maybe a third of what I lost. According to them, the place was empty when they hit it. Peg was out."

"And?"

"And I set them up. They hit the place, they carted everything away, and I came home with Peg and stabbed her six, eight times, whatever it was, and left her there so it'd look like it happened in a burglary."

"How could the burglars testify that you stabbed your wife?"

"They couldn't. All they said was they didn't and she wasn't home when they were there, and that I hired them to do the burglary. The cops pieced the rest of it together."

"What did they do, take you downtown?"

"No. They came over to the house, it was early, I don't know what time. It was the first I knew that the spics were arrested, let alone that they were trying to do a job on me. They just wanted to talk, the cops, and at first I talked to them, and then I started to get the drift of what they were trying to put on to me. So I said I wasn't saying anything more without my lawyer present, and I called him, and he left half his breakfast on the table and came over in a hurry, and he wouldn't let me say a word."

"And the cops didn't take you in or book you?"

"No."

"Did they buy your story?"

"No way. I didn't really tell 'em a story, because Kaplan wouldn't let me say anything. They didn't drag me in, because they don't have a case yet, but Kaplan says they're gonna be building one if they can. They told me not to leave town. You believe it? My wife's dead, the *Post* headline says, 'Quiz Husband in Burglary Murder,' and what the hell do they think I'm gonna do? Am I going fishing for fucking trout in Montana? 'Don't leave town.' You see this shit on television, you think nobody in real life talks this way. Maybe television's where they get it from."

I waited for him to tell me what he wanted from me. I didn't have long to wait.

"Why I called," he said, "is Kaplan wants to hire a detective. He figured maybe these guys talked around the neighborhood, maybe they bragged to their friends, maybe there's a way to prove they did the killing. He

93

says the cops won't concentrate on that end if they're too busy nailing the lid shut on me."

I explained that I didn't have any official standing, that I had no license and filed no reports.

"That's okay," he insisted. "I told Kaplan what I want is somebody I can trust, somebody who'll do the job for me. I don't think they're gonna have any kind of a case at all, Matt, but the longer this drags on, the worse it is for me. I want it cleared up, I want it in the papers that these Spanish assholes did it all and I had nothing to do with anything. You name a fair fee and I'll pay it, me to you, and it can be cash in your hand if you don't like checks. What do you say?"

He wanted somebody he could trust. Had Carolyn from the Caroline told him how trustworthy I was?

What did I say? I said yes.

I met Tommy Tillary and his lawyer in Drew Kaplan's office on Court Street, a few blocks from Brooklyn's Borough Hall. There was a Syrian restaurant next door and, at the corner, a grocery store specializing in Middle Eastern imports stood next to an antique shop overflowing with stripped-oak furniture and brass lamps and bedsteads. Kaplan's office ran to wood paneling and leather chairs and oak file cabinets. His name and the names of two partners were painted on the frosted-glass door in old-fashioned gold-and-black lettering. Kaplan himself looked conservatively up-to-date, with a three-piece striped suit that was better cut than mine. Tommy wore his burgundy blazer and gray-flannel trousers and loafers. Strain showed at the corners of his blue eyes and around his mouth. His complexion was off, too.

"All we want you to do," Kaplan said, "is find a key in one of their pants pockets, Herrera's or Cruz's, and trace it to a locker in Penn Station, and in the locker there's a footlong knife with their prints and her blood on it."

"Is that what it's going to take?"

He smiled. "It wouldn't hurt. No, actually, we're not in such bad shape. They got some shaky testimony from a pair of Latins who've been in and out of trouble since they got weaned to Tropicana. They got what looks to them like a good motive on Tommy's part."

"Which is?"

I was looking at Tommy when I asked. His eyes slipped away from mine. Kaplan said, "A marital triangle, a case of the shorts, and a strong money motive. Margaret Tillary inherited a little over a quarter of a million dollars six or eight months ago. An aunt left a million two and it got cut up four ways. What they don't bother to notice is he loved his wife, and how many husbands cheat? What is it they say — ninety percent cheat and ten percent lie?"

"That's good odds."

"One of the killers, Angel Herrera, did some odd jobs at the Tillary house last March or April. Spring cleaning; he hauled stuff out of the basement and attic, a little donkeywork. According to Herrera, that's how Tommy knew him to contact him about the burglary. According to common sense, that's how Herrera and his buddy Cruz knew the house and what was in it and how to gain access."

"The case against Tommy sounds pretty thin."

"It is," Kaplan said. "The thing is, you go to court with something like this and you lose even if you win. For the rest of your life, everybody remembers you stood trial for murdering your wife, never mind that you won an acquittal.

"Besides," he said, "you never know which way a jury's going to jump. Tommy's alibi is he was with another lady at the time of the burglary. The woman's a colleague; they could see it as completely aboveboard, but who says they're going to? What they sometimes do, they decide they don't believe the alibi because it's his girlfriend lying for him, and at the same time they label him a scumbag for screwing around while his wife's getting killed."

"You keep it up," Tommy said, "I'll find myself guilty, the way you make it sound."

"Plus he's hard to get a sympathetic jury for. He's a big handsome guy, a sharp dresser, and you'd love him in a gin joint, but how much do you love him in a courtroom? He's a securities salesman, he's beautiful on the phone, and that means every clown who ever lost a hundred dollars on a stock tip or bought magazines over the phone is going to walk into the courtroom with a hard-on for him. I'm telling you, I want to stay the hell out of court. I'll *win* in court, I know that, or the worst that'll happen is I'll win on appeal, but who needs it? This is a case that shouldn't be in the first place, and I'd love to clear it up before they even go so far as presenting a bill to the grand jury."

"So from me you want — "

"Whatever you can find, Matt. Whatever discredits Cruz and Herrera. I don't know what's there to be found, but you were a cop and now you're private, and you can get down in the streets and nose around."

I nodded. I could do that. "One thing," I said. "Wouldn't you be better off with a Spanish-speaking detective? I know enough to buy a beer in a bodega, but I'm a long way from fluent. "

Kaplan shook his head. "A personal relationship's worth more than a dime's worth of *'Me llamo Matteo y ¿como está usted?'* "

"That's the truth," Tommy Tillary said. "Matt, I know I can count on you."

I wanted to tell him all he could count on was his fingers. I didn't really see what I could expect to uncover that wouldn't turn up in a regular police investigation. But I'd spent enough time carrying a shield to know not to push away money when somebody wants to give it to you. I felt comfortable taking a fee. The man was inheriting a quarter of a million, plus whatever insurance his wife had carried. If he was willing to spread some of it around, I was willing to take it.

So I went to Sunset Park and spent some time in the streets and some more time in the bars. Sunset Park is in Brooklyn, of course, on the borough's western edge, above Bay Ridge and south and west of Green-Wood Cemetery. These days, there's a lot of brownstoning going on there, with young urban professionals renovating the old houses and gentrifying the neighborhood. Back then, the upwardly mobile young had not yet discovered Sunset Park, and the area was a mix of Latins and Scandinavians, most of the former Puerto Ricans, most of the latter Norwegians. The balance was gradually shifting from Europe to the islands, from light to dark, but this was a process that had been going on for ages and there was nothing hurried about it.

I talked to Herrera's landlord and Cruz's former employer and one of his recent girlfriends. I drank beer in bars and the back rooms of bodegas. I went to the local station house, I read the sheets on both of the burglars and drank coffee with the cops and picked up some of the stuff that doesn't get on the yellow sheets.

I found out that Miguelito Cruz had once killed a man in a tavern brawl over a woman. There were no charges pressed; a dozen witnesses reported that the dead man had gone after Cruz first with a broken bottle. Cruz had most likely been carrying the knife, but several witnesses insisted it had been tossed to him by an anonymous benefactor, and there hadn't been enough evidence to make a case of weapons possession, let alone homicide.

I learned that Herrera had three children living with their mother in Puerto Rico. He was divorced but wouldn't marry his current girlfriend because he regarded himself as still married to his ex-wife in the eyes of God. He sent money to his children when he had any to send.

I learned other things. They didn't seem terribly consequential then and they've faded from memory altogether by now, but I wrote them down in my pocket notebook as I learned them, and every day or so I duly reported my findings to Drew Kaplan. He always seemed pleased with what I told him.

I invariably managed a stop at Armstrong's before I called it a night. One night she was there, Carolyn Cheatham, drinking bourbon this time, her face frozen with stubborn old pain. It took her a blink or two to recognize me. Then tears started to form in the corners of her eyes, and she used the back of one hand to wipe them away.

I didn't approach her until she beckoned. She patted the stool beside hers and I eased myself onto it. I had coffee with bourbon in it and bought a refill for her. She was pretty drunk already, but that's never been enough reason to turn down a drink.

She talked about Tommy. He was being nice to her, she said. Calling up, sending flowers. But he wouldn't see her, because it wouldn't look right, not for a new widower, not for a man who'd been publicly accused of murder.

"He sends flowers with no card enclosed," she said. "He calls me from pay phones. The son of a bitch."

Billie called me aside. "I didn't want to put her out," he said, "a nice woman like that, shit-faced as she is. But I thought I was gonna have to. You'll see she gets home?"

I said I would.

I got her out of there and a cab came along and saved us the walk. At her place, I took the keys from her and unlocked the door. She half sat, half sprawled on the couch. I had to use the bathroom, and when I came back, her eyes were closed and she was snoring lightly.

I got her coat and shoes off, put her to bed, loosened her clothing, and covered her with a blanket. I was tired from all that and sat down on the couch for a minute, and I almost dozed off myself. Then I snapped awake and let myself out.

I went back to Sunset Park the next day. I learned that Cruz had been in trouble as a youth. With a gang of neighborhood kids, he used to go into the city and cruise Greenwich Village, looking for homosexuals to beat up. He'd had a dread of homosexuality, probably flowing as it generally does out of a fear of a part of himself, and he stifled that dread by fag-bashing.

"He still doan' like them," a woman told me. She had glossy black hair and opaque eyes, and she was letting me pay for her rum and orange juice. "He's pretty, you know, an' they come on to him, an' he doan' like it."

I called that item in, along with a few others equally earth-shaking. I bought myself a steak dinner at the Slate over on Tenth Avenue, then finished up at Armstrong's, not drinking very hard, just coasting along on bourbon and coffee.

Twice, the phone rang for me. Once, it was Tommy Tillary, telling me how much he appreciated what I was doing for him. It seemed to me that all I was doing was taking his money, but he had me believing that my loyalty and invaluable assistance were all he had to cling to.

The second call was from Carolyn. More praise. I was a gentleman, she assured me, and a hell of a fellow all around. And I should forget that she'd been bad-mouthing Tommy. Everything was going to be fine with them.

I took the next day off. I think I went to a movie, and it may have been *The Sting*, with Newman and Redford achieving vengeance through swindling.

The day after that, I did another tour of duty over in Brooklyn. And the day after that, I picked up the *News* first thing in the morning. The headline was nonspecific, something like KILL SUSPECT HANGS SELF IN CELL, but I knew it was my case before I turned to the story on page three.

Miguelito Cruz had torn his clothing into strips, knotted the strips together, stood his iron bedstead on its side, climbed onto it, looped his homemade rope around an overhead pipe, and jumped off the up-ended bedstead and into the next world.

That evening's six o'clock TV news had the rest of the story. Informed of his friend's death, Angel Herrera had recanted his original story and admitted that he and Cruz had conceived and executed the Tillary burglary on their own. It had been Miguelito who had stabbed the Tillary woman when she walked in on them. He'd picked up a kitchen knife while Herrera watched in horror. Miguelito always had a short temper, Herrera said, but they were friends, even cousins, and they had hatched their story to protect Miguelito. But now that he was dead, Herrera could admit what had really happened.

I was in Armstrong's that night, which was not remarkable. I had it in mind to get drunk, though I could not have told you why, and that was remarkable, if not unheard of. I got drunk a lot those days, but I rarely set out with that intention. I just wanted to feel a little better, a little more mellow, and somewhere along the way I'd wind up waxed.

I wasn't drinking particularly hard or fast, but I was working at it, and then somewhere around ten or eleven the door opened and I knew who it was before I turned around. Tommy Tillary, well dressed and freshly barbered, making his first appearance in Jimmy's place since his wife was killed.

"Hey, look who's here!" he called out, and grinned that big grin. People rushed over to shake his hand. Billie was behind the stick, and he'd no sooner set one up on the house for our hero than Tommy insisted on buying a round for the bar. It was an expensive gesture — there must have been thirty or forty people in there — but I don't think he cared if there were three hundred or four hundred.

I stayed where I was, letting the others mob him, but he worked his way over to me and got an arm around my shoulders. "This is the man," he announced. "Best fucking detective ever wore out a pair of shoes. This man's money," he told Billie, "is no good at all tonight.

He can't buy a drink; he can't buy a cup of coffee; if you went and put in pay toilets since I was last here, he can't use his own dime."

"The john's still free," Billie said, "but don't give the boss any ideas."

"Oh, don't tell me he didn't already think of it," Tommy said. "Matt, my boy, I love you. I was in a tight spot, I didn't want to walk out of my house, and you came through for me."

What the hell had I done? I hadn't hanged Miguelito Cruz or coaxed a confession out of Angel Herrera. I hadn't even set eyes on either man. But he was buying the drinks, and I had a thirst, so who was I to argue?

I don't know how long we stayed there. Curiously, my drinking slowed down even as Tommy's picked up speed. Carolyn, I noticed, was not present, nor did her name find its way into the conversation. I wondered if she would walk in — it was, after all, her neighborhood bar, and she was apt to drop in on her own. I wondered what would happen if she did.

I guess there were a lot of things I wondered about, and perhaps that's what put the brakes on my own drinking. I didn't want any gaps in my memory, any gray patches in my awareness.

After a while, Tommy was hustling me out of Armstrong's. "This is celebration time," he told me. "We don't want to sit in one place till we grow roots. We want to bop a little."

He had a car, and I just went along with him without paying too much attention to exactly where we were. We went to a noisy Greek club on the East Side, I think, where the waiters looked like Mob hit men. We went to a couple of trendy singles joints. We wound up somewhere in the Village, in a dark, beery cave.

It was quiet there, and conversation was possible, and I found myself asking him what I'd done that was so praiseworthy. One man had killed himself and another had confessed, and where was my role in either incident?

"The stuff you came up with," he said.

"What stuff? I should have brought back fingernail parings, you could have had someone work voodoo on them."

"About Cruz and the fairies."

"He was up for murder. He didn't kill himself because he was afraid they'd get him for fag-bashing when he was a juvenile offender."

Tommy took a sip of scotch. He said, "Couple days ago, huge black guy comes up to Cruz in the chow line. 'Wait'll you get up to Green Haven,' he tells him. 'Every blood there's gonna have you for a girlfriend. Doctor gonna have to cut you a brand-new asshole, time you get outa there.' "

I didn't say anything.

"Kaplan," he said. "Drew talked to somebody who talked to somebody, and that did it. Cruz took a good look at the idea of playin' drop the soap for half the jigs in captivity, and the next thing you know, the murderous little bastard was dancing on air. And good riddance to him."

I couldn't seem to catch my breath. I worked on it while Tommy went to the bar for another round. I hadn't touched the drink in front of me, but I let him buy for both of us.

When he got back, I said, "Herrera."

"Changed his story. Made a full confession."

"And pinned the killing on Cruz."

"Why not? Cruz wasn't around to complain. Who knows which one of 'em did it, and for that matter, who cares? The thing is, you gave us the lever."

"For Cruz," I said. "To get him to kill himself."

"And for Herrera. Those kids of his in Santurce.

Drew spoke to Herrera's lawyer and Herrera's lawyer spoke to Herrera, and the message was, 'Look, you're going up for burglary whatever you do, and probably for murder; but if you tell the right story, you'll draw shorter time, and on top of that, that nice Mr. Tillary's gonna let bygones be bygones and every month there's a nice check for your wife and kiddies back home in Puerto Rico.' "

At the bar, a couple of old men were reliving the Louis-Schmeling fight, the second one, where Louis punished the German champion. One of the old fellows was throwing roundhouse punches in the air, demonstrating.

I said, "Who killed your wife?"

"One or the other of them. If I had to bet, I'd say Cruz. He had those little beady eyes; you looked at him up close and you got that he was a killer."

"When did you look at him up close?"

"When they came and cleaned the house, the basement, and the attic. Not when they came and cleaned me out; that was the second time."

He smiled, but I kept looking at him until the smile lost its certainty. "That was Herrera who helped around the house," I said. "You never met Cruz."

"Cruz came along, gave him a hand."

"You never mentioned that before."

"Oh, sure I did, Matt. What difference does it make, anyway?"

"Who killed her, Tommy?"

"Hey, let it alone, huh?"

"Answer the question."

"I already answered it."

"You killed her, didn't you?"

"What are you, crazy? Cruz killed her and Herrera swore to it, isn't that enough for you?"

"Tell me you didn't kill her."

"I didn't kill her."

"Tell me again."

"I didn't fucking kill her. What's the matter with you?"

"I don't believe you."

"Oh, Jesus," he said. He closed his eyes, put his head in his hands. He sighed and looked up and said, "You know, it's a funny thing with me. Over the telephone, I'm the best salesman you could ever imagine. I swear I could sell sand to the Arabs, I could sell ice in the winter, but face-to-face I'm no good at all. Why do you figure that is?"

"You tell me."

"I don't know. I used to think it was my face, the eyes and the mouth; I don't know. It's easy over the phone. I'm talking to a stranger, I don't know who he is or what he looks like, and he's not lookin' at me, and it's a cinch. Face-to-face, especially with someone I know, it's a different story." He looked at me. "If we were doin' this over the phone, you'd buy the whole thing."

"It's possible."

"It's fucking certain. Word for word, you'd buy the package. Suppose I was to tell you I did kill her, Matt. You couldn't prove anything. Look, the both of us walked in there, the place was a mess from the burglary, we got in an argument, tempers flared, something happened."

"You set up the burglary. You planned the whole thing, just the way Cruz and Herrera accused you of doing. And now you wriggled out of it."

"And you helped me — don't forget that part of it."

"I won't."

"And I wouldn't have gone away for it anyway, Matt. Not a chance. I'da beat it in court, only this way I don't have to go to court. Look, this is just the booze talkin', and we can forget it in the morning, right? I didn't kill her, you didn't accuse me, we're still buddies, everything's fine. Right?"

Blackouts are never there when you want them. I woke up the next day and remembered all of it, and I found myself wishing I didn't. He'd killed his wife and he was getting away with it. And I'd helped him. I'd taken his money, and in return I'd shown him how to set one man up for suicide and pressure another into making a false confession.

And what was I going to do about it?

I couldn't think of a thing. Any story I carried to the police would be speedily denied by Tommy and his lawyer, and all I had was the thinnest of hearsay evidence, my own client's own words when he and I both had a skinful of booze. I went over it for a few days, looking for ways to shake something loose, and there was nothing. I could maybe interest a newspaper reporter, maybe get Tommy some press coverage that wouldn't make him happy, but why? And to what purpose?

It rankled. But I would just have a couple of drinks, and then it wouldn't rankle so much.

Angel Herrera pleaded guilty to burglary, and in return the Brooklyn D.A.'s Office dropped all homicide charges. He went upstate to serve five to ten.

And then I got a call in the middle of the night. I'd been sleeping a couple of hours, but the phone woke me and I groped for it. It took me a minute to recognize the voice on the other end.

It was Carolyn Cheatham.

"I had to call you," she said, "on account of you're a bourbon man and a gentleman. I owed it to you to call you."

"What's the matter?"

"He ditched me," she said, "and he got me fired out of Tannahill and Company so he won't have to look at me around the office. Once he didn't need me to back up his story, he let go of me, and do you know he did it over the phone?"

"Carolyn — "

"It's all in the note," she said. "I'm leaving a note."

"Look, don't do anything yet," I said. I was out of bed, fumbling for my clothes. "I'll be right over. We'll talk about it."

"You can't stop me, Matt."

"I won't try to stop you. We'll talk first, and then you can do anything you want."

The phone clicked in my ear.

I threw my clothes on, rushed over there, hoping it would be pills, something that took its time. I broke a small pane of glass in the downstairs door and let myself in, then used an old credit card to slip the bolt of her spring lock.

The room smelled of cordite. She was on the couch she'd passed out on the last time I saw her. The gun was still in her hand, limp at her side, and there was a black-rimmed hole in her temple.

There was a note, too. An empty bottle of Maker's Mark stood on the coffee table, an empty glass beside it. The booze showed in her handwriting and in the sullen phrasing of the suicide note.

I read the note. I stood there for a few minutes, not for very long, and then I got a dish towel from the Pullman kitchen and wiped the bottle and the glass. I took another matching glass, rinsed it out and wiped it, and put it in the drainboard of the sink.

I stuffed the note in my pocket. I took the gun from her fingers, checked routinely for a pulse, then wrapped a sofa pillow around the gun to muffle its report. I fired one round into her chest, another into her open mouth.

I dropped the gun into a pocket and left.

They found the gun in Tommy Tillary's house, stuffed between the cushions of the living-room sofa, clean of prints inside and out. Ballistics got a perfect match. I'd aimed for soft tissue with the round shot into her chest, because bullets can fragment on impact with bone. That was one reason I'd fired the extra shots. The other was to rule out the possibility of suicide.

After the story made the papers, I picked up the phone and called Drew Kaplan. "I don't understand it," I said. "He was free and clear; why the hell did he kill the girl?"

"Ask him yourself," Kaplan said. He did not sound happy. "You want my opinion, he's a lunatic. I honestly didn't think he was. I figured maybe he killed his wife, maybe he didn't. Not my job to try him. But I didn't figure he was a homicidal maniac."

"It's certain he killed the girl?"

"Not much question. The gun's pretty strong evidence. Talk about finding somebody with the smoking pistol in his hand, here it was in Tommy's couch. The idiot."

"Funny he kept it."

"Maybe he had other people he wanted to shoot. Go figure a crazy man. No, the gun's evidence, and there was a phone tip — a man called in the shooting, reported a man running out of there, and gave a description that fitted Tommy pretty well. Even had him wearing that red blazer he nears, tacky thing makes him look like an usher at the Paramount."

"It sounds tough to square."

"Well, somebody else'll have to try to do it," Kaplan said. "I told him I can't defend him this time. What it amounts to, I wash my hands of him."

I thought of that when I read that Angel Herrera got out just the other day. He served all ten years because he was as good at getting into trouble inside the walls as he'd been on the outside.

Somebody killed Tommy Tillary with a homemade knife after he'd served two years and three months of a manslaughter stretch. I wondered at the time if that was Herrera getting even, and I don't suppose I'll ever know. Maybe the checks stopped going to Santurce and Herrera took it the wrong way. Or maybe Tommy said the wrong thing to somebody else and said it face-to-face instead of over the phone.

I don't think I'd do it that way now. I don't drink anymore, and the impulse to play God seems to have evaporated with the booze.

But then, a lot of things have changed. Billie left Armstrong's not long after that, left New York, too; the last I heard he was off drink himself, living in Sausalito and making candles. I ran into Dennis the other day in a bookstore on lower Fifth Avenue full of odd volumes on yoga and spiritualism and holistic healing. And Armstrong's is scheduled to close the end of next month. The lease is up for renewal, and I suppose the next you know, the old joint'll be another Korean fruit market.

I still light a candle now and then for Carolyn Cheatham and Miguelito Cruz. Not often. Just every once in a while.

BATMAN'S HELPERS

Reliable's offices are in the Flatiron Building, at Broadway and Twenty-third. The receptionist, an elegant black girl with high cheekbones and processed hair, gave me a nod and a smile, and I went on down the hall to Wally Witt's office.

He was at his desk, a short stocky man with a bulldog jaw and gray hair cropped close to his head. Without rising he said, "Matt, good to see you, you're right on time. You know these guys? Matt Scudder, Jimmy diSalvo, Lee Trombauer." We shook hands all around. "We're waiting on Eddie Rankin. Then we can go out there and protect the integrity of the American merchandising system."

"Can't do that without Eddie," Jimmy diSalvo said.

"No, we need him," Wally said. "He's our pit bull. He's attack-trained, Eddie is."

He came through the door a few minutes later and I saw what they meant. Without looking alike, Jimmy and Wally and Lee all looked like ex-cops, as I suppose do I. Eddie Rankin looked like the kind of guy we used to have to bring in on a bad Saturday night. He was a big man, broad in the shoulders, narrow in the waist. His hair was blond, almost white, and he wore it short at the sides but long in back. It lay on his neck like a mane. He had a broad forehead and a pug nose. His complexion was very fair and his full lips were intensely red, almost artificially so. He looked like a roughneck, and you sensed that his response to any sort of stress was likely to be physical, and abrupt.

Wally Witt introduced him to me. The others already knew him. Eddie Rankin shook my hand and his left hand fastened on my shoulder and gave a squeeze. "Hey, Matt," he said. "Pleased to meetcha. Whattaya say, guys, we ready to come to the aid of the Caped Crusader?"

Jimmy diSalvo started whistling the theme from *Batman*, the old television show. Wally said, "Okay, who's packing? Is everybody packing?"

Lee Trombauer drew back his suit jacket to show a revolver in a shoulder rig. Eddie Rankin took out a large automatic and laid it on Wally's desk. "Batman's gun," he announced.

"Batman don't carry a gun," Jimmy told him.

"Then he better stay outta New York," Eddie said. "Or he'll get his ass shot off. Those revolvers, I wouldn't carry one of them on a bet."

"This shoots as straight as what you got," Lee said. "And it won't jam."

"This baby don't jam," Eddie said. He picked up the automatic and held it out for display. "You got a revolver," he said, "a .38, whatever you got — "

"A .38."

"— and a guy takes it away from you, all he's gotta do is point it and shoot it. Even if he never saw a gun before, he knows how to do that much. This monster, though" — and he demonstrated, flicking the safety, working the slide — "all this shit you gotta go through, before he can figure it out I got the gun away from him and I'm making him eat it."

"Nobody's taking my gun away from me," Lee said.

"What everybody says, but look at all the times it happens. Cop gets shot with his own gun, nine times out of ten it's a revolver."

"That's because that's all they carry," Lee said.

"Well, there you go."

Jimmy and I weren't carrying guns. Wally offered to equip us but we both declined. "Not that anybody's likely to have to show a piece, let alone use one, God forbid," Wally said. "But it can get nasty out there and it helps to have the feeling of authority. Well, let's go get 'em, huh? The Batmobile's waiting at the curb."

We rode down in the elevator, five grown men, three of us armed with handguns. Eddie Rankin had on a plaid sport jacket and khaki trousers. The rest of us wore suits and ties. We went out the Fifth Avenue exit and followed Wally to his car, a five-year-old Fleetwood Cadillac parked next to a hydrant. There were no tickets on the windshield; a PBA courtesy card had kept the traffic cops at bay.

Wally drove and Eddie Rankin sat in front with him. The rest of us rode in back. We cruised up Sixth to Fifty-fourth Street and turned right, and Wally parked next to a hydrant a few doors from Fifth. We walked together to the corner of Fifth and turned downtown. Near the middle of the block a trio of black men had set up shop as sidewalk vendors. One had a display of women's handbags and silk scarves, all arranged neatly on top of a folding card table. The other two were offering T-shirts and cassette tapes.

In an undertone Wally said, "Here we go. These three were here yesterday. Matt, why don't you and Lee check down the block, make sure those two down at the corner don't have what we're looking for. Then double back and we'll take these dudes off. Meanwhile I'll let the man sell me a shirt."

Lee and I walked down to the corner. The two vendors in question were selling books. We established this and headed back. "Real police work," I said.

"Be grateful we don't have to fill out a report, list the titles of the books."

"The alleged books."

When we rejoined the others Wally was holding an oversize T-shirt to his chest, modeling it for us. "What do you say?" he demanded. "Is it me? Do you think it's me?"

"I think it's the Joker," Jimmy diSalvo said.

"That's what I think," Wally said. He looked at the two Africans, who were smiling uncertainly. "I think it's a violation, is what I think. I think we got to confiscate all the Batman stuff. It's unauthorized, it's an illegal violation of copyright protection, it's unlicensed, and we got to take it in."

The two vendors had stopped smiling, but they didn't seem to have a very clear idea of what was going on. Off to the side, the third man, the fellow with the scarves and purses, was looking wary.

"You speak English?" Wally asked them.

"They speak numbers," Jimmy said. " 'Fi dollah, ten dollah, please, thank you.' That's what they speak."

"Where you from?" Wally demanded. "Senegal, right? Dakar. You from Dakar?"

They nodded, brightening at words they recognized. "Dakar," one of them echoed. Both of them were wearing Western clothes, but they looked faintly foreign — loose-fitting long-sleeved shirts with long pointed collars and a glossy finish, baggy pleated pants. Loafers with leather mesh tops.

"What do you speak?" Wally asked. "You speak French? Parley-voo *Français*?" The one who'd spoken before replied now in a torrent of French, and Wally backed away from him and shook his head. "I don't know why the hell I asked," he said. "Parley-voo's all I know of the fucking language." To the Africans he said, "Police. You parley-voo that? Police. *Policia.* You capeesh?" He opened his wallet and showed them some sort of badge. "No sell Batman," he said, waving one of the shirts at them. "Batman no good. It's unauthorized, it's not made under a licensing agreement, and you can't sell it."

"No Batman," one of them said.

"Jesus, don't tell me I'm getting through to them. Right, no Batman. No, put your money away, I can't take a bribe, I'm not with the department no more. All I want's the Batman stuff. You can keep the rest."

All but a handful of their T-shirts were unauthorized Batman items. The rest showed Walt Disney characters, themselves almost certainly as unauthorized as the Batman merchandise, but Disney wasn't Reliable's client today so it was none of our concern. While we loaded up with Batman and the Joker, Eddie Rankin looked through the cassettes, then pawed through the silk scarves the third vendor had on display. He let the man keep the scarves, but he took a purse, snakeskin by the look of it. "No good," he told the man, who nodded, expressionless.

We trooped back to the Fleetwood and Wally popped the trunk. We deposited the confiscated T's between the spare tire and some loose fishing tackle. "Don't worry if the shit gets dirty," Wally said. "It's all gonna be destroyed anyway. Eddie, you start carrying a purse, people are gonna say things."

"Woman I know," he said, "she'll like this." He wrapped the purse in a Batman T-shirt and placed it in the trunk.

"Okay," Wally said. "That went real smooth. What we'll do now, Lee, you and Matt take the east side of

Fifth and the rest of us'll stay on this side and we'll work our way down to Forty-second. I don't know if we'll get much, because even if they can't speak English they can sure get the word around fast, but we'll make sure there's no unlicensed Batcrap on the avenue before we move on. We'll maintain eye contact back and forth across the street, and if you hit anything give the high sign and we'll converge and take 'em down. Everybody got it?"

Everybody seemed to. We left the car with its trunkful of contraband and returned to Fifth Avenue. The two T-shirt vendors from Dakar had packed up and disappeared; they'd have to find something else to sell and someplace else to sell it. The man with the scarves and purses was still doing business. He froze when he caught sight of us.

"No Batman," Wally told him.

"No Batman," he echoed.

"I'll be a son of a bitch," Wally said. "The guy's learning English."

Lee and I crossed the street and worked our way downtown. There were vendors all over the place, offering clothing and tapes and small appliances and books and fast food. Most of them didn't have the peddler's license the law required, and periodically the city would sweep the streets, especially the main commercial avenues, rounding them up and fining them and confiscating their stock. Then after a week or so the cops would stop trying to enforce a basically unenforceable law, and the peddlers would be back in business again.

It was an apparently endless cycle, but the booksellers were exempt from it.

The court had decided that the First Amendment embodied in its protection of freedom of the press the right of anyone to sell printed matter on the street, so if you had books for sale you never got hassled. As a result, a lot of scholarly antiquarian booksellers offered their wares on the city streets. So did any number of illiterates hawking remaindered art books and stolen best-sellers, along with homeless street people who rescued old magazines from people's garbage cans and spread them out on the pavement, living in hope that someone would want to buy them.

In front of St. Patrick's Cathedral we found a Pakistani with T-shirts and sweatshirts. I asked him if he had any Batman merchandise and he went right through the piles himself and pulled out half a dozen items. We didn't bother signaling the cavalry across the street. Lee just showed the man a badge — Special Officer, it said — and I explained that we had to confiscate Batman items.

"He is the big seller, Batman," the man said. "I get Batman, I sell him fast as I can."

"Well, you better not sell him anymore," I said, "because it's against the law."

"Excuse, please," he said. "What is law? Why is Batman against law? Is my understanding Batman is *for* law. He is good guy, is it not so?"

I explained about copyright and trademarks and licensing agreements. It was a little bit like explaining the internal-combustion engine to a field mouse. He kept nodding his head, but I don't know how much of it he got. He understood the main point — that we were walking off with his stock, and he was stuck for whatever it cost him. He didn't like that part but there wasn't much he could do about it.

Lee tucked the shirts under his arm and we kept going. At Forty-seventh Street we crossed over in response to a signal from Wally. They'd found another pair of Senegalese with a big spread of Batman items — T's and sweatshirts and gimme caps and sun visors, some a direct knockoff of the copyrighted Bat signal, others a variation on the theme, but none of it authorized and all of it subject to confiscation. The two men — they looked like brothers, and were dressed identically in baggy beige trousers and sky-blue nylon shirts — couldn't understand what was wrong with their merchandise and couldn't believe we intended to haul it all away with us. But there were five of us, and we were large intimidating white men with an authoritarian manner, and what could they do about it?

"I'll get the car," Wally said. "No way we're gonna schlep this crap seven blocks in this heat."

With the trunk almost full, we drove to Thirty-fourth and broke for lunch at a place Wally liked. We sat at a large round table. Ornate beer steins hung from the beams overhead. We had a round of drinks, then ordered sandwiches and fries and half-liter steins of dark beer. I had a Coke to start, another Coke with the food, and coffee afterward.

"You're not drinking," Lee Trombauer said.

"Not today."

"Not on duty," Jimmy said, and everybody laughed.

"What I want to know," Eddie Rankin said, "is why everybody wants a fucking Batman shirt in the first place."

"Not just shirts," somebody said.

"Shirts, sweaters, caps, lunch boxes, if you could print it on Tampax they'd be shoving 'em up their twats. Why Batman, for Christ's sake?"

"It's hot," Wally said.

" 'It's hot.' What the fuck does that mean?"

"It means it's hot. That's what it means. It's hot means it's hot. Everybody wants it because everybody else wants it, and that means it's hot."

"I seen the movie," Eddie said. "You see it?"

Two of us had, two of us hadn't.

"It's okay," he said. "Basically I'd say it's a kid's movie, but it's okay."

"So?"

"So how many T-shirts in extra large do you sell to kids? Everybody's buying this shit, and all you can tell me is it's hot because it's hot. I don't get it."

"You don't have to," Wally said. "It's the same as the niggers. You want to try explaining to them why they can't sell Batman unless there's a little copyright notice printed under the design? While you're at it, you can explain to me why the assholes counterfeiting the crap don't counterfeit the copyright notice while they're at it. The thing is, nobody has to do any explaining because nobody has to understand. The only message they have to get on the street is Batman no good, no sell Batman. If they learn that much we're doing our job right."

Wally paid for everybody's lunch. We stopped at the Flatiron Building long enough to empty the trunk and carry everything upstairs, then drove down to the Village and worked the sidewalk market on Sixth Avenue below Eighth Street. We made a few confiscations without incident. Then, near the subway entrance at West Third, we were taking a dozen shirts and about as many visors from a West Indian when another vendor decided to get into the act. He was wearing a dashiki and had his hair in Rastafarian dreadlocks, and he said, "You can't take the brother's wares, man. You can't do that."

"It's unlicensed merchandise produced in contravention of international copyright protection," Wally told him.

"Maybe so," the man said, "but that don't empower you to seize it. Where's your due process? Where's your authority? You aren't police." Poe-lease, he said, bearing down on the first syllable. "You can't come into a man's store, seize his wares."

"Store?" Eddie Rankin moved toward him, his hands hovering at his sides. "You see a store here? All I see's a lot of fucking shit in the middle of a fucking blanket."

"This is the man's store. This is the man's place of business."

"And what's this?" Eddie demanded. He walked over to the right, where the man with the dreadlocks had stick incense displayed for sale on a pair of upended orange crates. "This your store?"

"That's right. It's my store."

"You know what it looks like to me? It looks like you're selling drug paraphernalia. That's what it looks like."

"It's incense," the Rasta said. "For bad smells."

"Bad smells," Eddie said. One of the sticks of incense was smoldering, and Eddie picked it up and sniffed at it. "Whew," he said. "That's a bad smell, I'll give you that. Smells like the catbox caught on fire."

The Rasta snatched the incense from him. "It's a good smell," he said. "Smells like your mama."

Eddie smiled at him, his red lips parting to show stained teeth. He looked happy, and very dangerous. "Say I kick your store into the middle of the street," he said, "and you with it. How's that sound to you?"

Smoothly, easily, Wally Witt moved between them. "Eddie," he said softly, and Eddie backed off and let the smile fade on his lips. To the incense seller Wally said, "Look, you and I got no quarrel with each other. I got a job to do and you got your own business to run."

"The brother here's got a business to run, too."

"Well, he's gonna have to run it without Batman, because that's how the law reads. But if you want to *be* Batman, playing the dozens with my man here and pushing into what doesn't concern you, then I got no choice. You follow me?"

"All I'm saying, I'm saying you want to confiscate the man's merchandise, you need you a policeman and a court order, something to make it official."

"Fine," Wally said. "You're saying it and I hear you saying it, but what I'm saying is all I need to do it is to do it, official or not. Now if you want to get a cop to stop me, fine, go ahead and do it, but as soon as you do I'm going to press charges for selling drug paraphernalia and operating without a peddler's license — "

"This here ain't drug paraphernalia, man. We both know that."

"We both know you're just trying to be a hard-on, and we both know what it'll get you. That what you want?"

The incense seller stood there for a moment, then dropped his eyes. "Don't matter what I want," he said.

"Well, you got that right," Wally told him. "It don't matter what you want."

We tossed the shirts and visors into the trunk and got out of there. On the way over to Astor Place Eddie said, "You didn't have to jump in there. I wasn't about to lose it."

"Never said you were."

"That mama stuff doesn't bother me. It's just nigger talk, they all talk that shit."

"I know."

"They'd talk about their fathers, but they don't know who the fuck they are, so they're stuck with their mothers. Bad smells, I shoulda stuck that shit up his ass, get right where the bad smells are. I hate a guy sticks his nose in like that."

"Your basic sidewalk lawyer."

"Basic asshole's what he is. Maybe I'll go back, talk with him later."

"On your own time."

"On my own time is right."

Astor Place hosts a more freewheeling street market, with a lot of Bowery types offering a mix of salvaged trash and stolen goods. There was something especially curious about our role, as we passed over hot radios and typewriters and jewelry and sought only merchandise that had been legitimately purchased, albeit from illegitimate manufacturers. We didn't find much Batman ware on display, although a lot of people, buyers and sellers alike, were wearing the Caped Crusader. We weren't about to strip the shirt off anybody's person, nor did we look too hard for contraband merchandise; the place was teeming with crackheads and crazies, and it was no time to push our luck.

"Let's get out of here," Wally said. "I hate to leave the car in this neighborhood. We already gave the client his money's worth."

By four we were back in Wally's office and his desk was heaped high with the fruits of our labors. "Look at all this shit," he said. "Today's trash and tomorrow's treasures. Twenty years and they'll be auctioning this crap at Christie's. Not this particular crap, because I'll messenger it over to the client and he'll chuck it in the incinerator. Gentlemen, you did a good day's work." He took out his wallet and gave each of the four of us a hundred-dollar bill. He said, "Same time tomorrow? Except I think we'll make lunch Chinese tomorrow. Eddie, don't forget your purse."

"Don't worry."

"Thing is you don't want to carry it if you go back to see your Rastafarian friend. He might get the wrong idea."

"Fuck him," Eddie said. "I got no time for him. He wants that incense up his ass, he's gonna have to stick it there himself."

Lee and Jimmy and Eddie went out, laughing, joking, slapping backs. I started out after them, then doubled back and asked Wally if he had a minute.

"Sure," he said. "Jesus, I don't believe this. Look."

"It's a Batman shirt."

"No shit, Sherlock. And look what's printed right under the Bat signal."

"The copyright notice."

"Right, which makes it a legal shirt. We got any more of these? No, no, no, no. Wait a minute, here's one. Here's another. Jesus, this is amazing. There any more? I don't see any others, do you?"

We went through the pile without finding more of the shirts with the copyright notice.

"Three," he said. "Well, that's not so bad. A mere fraction." He balled up the three shirts, dropped them back on the pile. "You want one of these? It's legit, you can wear it without fear of confiscation."

"I don't think so."

"You got kids? Take something home for your kids."

"One's in college and the other's in the service. I don't think they'd be interested. "

"Probably not." He stepped out from behind his desk. "Well, it went all right out there, don't you think? We had a good crew, worked well together."

"I guess."

"What's the matter, Matt?"

"Nothing, really. But I don't think I can make it tomorrow."

"No? Why's that?"

"Well, for openers, I've got a dentist appointment."

"Oh, yeah? What time?"

"Nine-fifteen."

"So how long can that take? Half an hour, an hour tops? Meet us here ten-thirty, that's good enough. The client doesn't have to know what time we hit the street."

"It's not just the dentist appointment, Wally."

"Oh?"

"I don't think I want to do this stuff anymore."

"What stuff? Copyright and trademark protection?"

"Yeah."

"What's the matter? It's beneath you? Doesn't make full use of your talents as a detective?"

"It's not that."

"Because it's not a bad deal for the money, seems to me. Hundred bucks for a short day, ten to four, hour and a half off for lunch with the lunch all paid for. You're a cheap lunch date, you don't drink, but even so. Call it a ten-dollar lunch, that's a hundred and ten dollars for what, four and a half hours' work?" He punched numbers on a desk top calculator. "That's $24.44 an hour. That's not bad wages. You want to take home better than that, you need either burglar's tools or a law degree, seems to me."

"The money's fine, Wally."

"Then what's the problem?"

I shook my head. "I just haven't got the heart for it," I said. "Hassling people who don't even speak the language, taking their goods from them because we're stronger than they are and there's nothing they can do about it."

"They can quit selling contraband, that's what they can do."

"How? They don't even know what's contraband."

"Well, that's where we come in. We're giving them an education. How they gonna learn if nobody teaches 'em?"

I'd loosened my tie earlier. Now I took it off, folded it, put it in my pocket.

He said, "Company owns a copyright, they got a right to control who uses it. Somebody else enters into a licensing agreement, pays money for the right to produce a particular item, they got a right to the exclusivity they paid for."

"I don't have a problem with that."

"So?"

"They don't even speak the language," I said.

He stood up straight. "Then who told 'em to come here?" he wanted to know. "Who fucking invited them? You can't walk a block in midtown without tripping over another super-salesman from Senegal. They swarm off that Air Afrique flight from Dakar and first thing you know they got an open-air store on world-famous Fifth Avenue. They don't pay rent, they don't pay taxes, they just spread a blanket on the concrete and rake in the dollars."

"They didn't look as though they were getting rich."

"They must do all right. Pay two bucks for a scarf and sell it for ten, they must come out okay. They stay at hotels like the Bryant, pack together like sardines, six or eight to the room. Sleep in shifts, cook their food on hot plates. Two, three months of that and it's back to fucking Dakar. They drop off the money, take a few minutes to get another baby started, then they're winging back to JFK to start all over again. You think we need that? Haven't we got enough spades of our own can't make a living, we got to fly in more of them?"

I sifted through the pile on his desk, picked up a sun visor with the Joker depicted on it. I wondered why anybody would want something like that. I said, "What do you figure it adds up to, the stuff we confiscated? A couple of hundred?"

"Jesus, I don't know. Figure ten for a T-shirt, and we got what, thirty or forty of them? Add in the sweatshirts, the rest of the shit, I bet it comes to close to a grand. Why?"

"I was just thinking. You paid us a hundred a man, plus whatever lunch came to."

"Eighty with the tip. What's the point?"

"You must have billed us to the client at what, fifty dollars an hour?"

"I haven't billed anything to anybody yet, I just walked in the door, but yes, that's the rate."

"How will you figure it, four men at eight hours a man?"

"Seven hours. We don't bill for lunchtime."

Seven hours seemed ample, considering that we'd worked four and a half. I said, "Seven times fifty times four of us is what? Fourteen-hundred dollars? Plus your own time, of course, and you must bill yourself at more than regular operative's rates. A hundred an hour?"

"Seventy-five."

"For seven hours is what, five hundred?"

"Five and a quarter," he said evenly.

"Plus fourteen hundred is nineteen and a quarter. Call it two thousand dollars to the client. Is that about right?"

"What are you saying, Matt? The client pays too much or you're not getting a big enough piece of the pie?"

"Neither. But if he wants to load up on this garbage" — I waved a hand at the heap on the desk — "wouldn't he be better off buying retail? Get a lot more bang for the buck, wouldn't he?"

He just stared at me for a long moment. Then, abruptly, his hard face cracked and he started to laugh. I was laughing, too, and it took all the tension out of the air. "Jesus, you're right," he said. "Guy's paying way too much."

"I mean, if you wanted to handle it for him, you wouldn't need to hire me and the other guys."

"I could just go around and pay cash."

"Right."

"I could even pass up the street guys altogether, go straight to the wholesaler."

"Save a dollar that way."

"I love it," he said. "You know what it sounds like? Sounds like something the federal government would do, get cocaine off the streets by buying it straight from the Colombians. Wait a minute, didn't they actually do something like that once?"

"I think so, but I don't think it was cocaine."

"No, it was opium. It was some years ago, they bought the entire Turkish opium crop because it was supposed to be the cheapest way to keep it out of the country. Bought it and burned it, and that, boys and girls, that was the end of heroin addiction in America."

"Worked like a charm, didn't it?"

"Nothing works," he said. "First principle of modern law enforcement. Nothing ever works. Funny thing is, in this case the client's not getting a bad deal. You own a copyright or a trademark, you got to defend it. Otherwise you risk losing it. You got to be able to say on such-and-such a date you paid so many dollars to defend your interests, and investigators acting as your agents confiscated so many items from so many merchants. And it's worth what you budget for it. Believe me, these big companies, they wouldn't spend the money year in and year out if they didn't figure it was worth it."

"I believe it," I said. "Anyway, I wouldn't lose a whole lot of sleep over the client getting screwed a little."

"You just don't like the work."

"I'm afraid not."

He shrugged. "I don't blame you. It's chickenshit.

But Jesus, Matt, most P.I. work is chickenshit. Was it that different in the department? Or on any police force? Most of what we did was chickenshit."

"And paperwork."

"And paperwork, you're absolutely right. Do some chickenshit and then write it up. And make copies."

"I can put up with a certain amount of chickenshit," I said. "But I honestly don't have the heart for what we did today. I felt like a bully."

"Listen, I'd rather be kicking in doors, taking down bad guys. That what you want?"

"Not really."

"Be Batman, tooling around Gotham City, righting wrongs. Do the whole thing not even carrying a gun. You know what they didn't have in the movie?"

"I haven't seen it yet."

"Robin, they didn't have Robin. Robin the Boy Wonder. He's not in the comic book anymore, either. Somebody told me they took a poll, had their readers call a nine-hundred number and vote, should they keep Robin or should they kill him. Like in ancient Rome, those fights, what do you call them?"

"Gladiators."

"Right. Thumbs-up or thumbs-down, and Robin got thumbs-down, so they killed him. Can you believe that?"

"I can believe anything."

"Yeah, you and me both. I always thought they were fags." I looked at him. "Batman and Robin, I mean. His *ward*, for Christ's sake. Playing dress-up, flying around, costumes, I figured it's gotta be some kind of fag S-and-M thing. Isn't that what you figured?"

"I never thought about it."

"Well, I never stayed up nights over it myself, but what else would it be? Anyway, he's dead now, Robin is.

Died of AIDS, I suppose, but the family's denying it, like What'shisname. You know who I mean."

I didn't, but I nodded.

"You gotta make a living, you know. Gotta turn a buck, whether it's hassling Africans or squatting out there on a blanket your own self, selling tapes and scarves. Fi' dollah, ten dollah." He looked at me. "No good, huh?"

"I don't think so, Wally."

"Don't want to be one of Batman's helpers. Well, you can't do what you can't do. What the fuck do I know about it, anyway? You don't drink. I don't have a problem with it, myself. But if I couldn't put my feet up at the end of the day, have a few pops, who knows? Maybe I couldn't do it either. Matt, you're a good man. If you change your mind — "

"I know. Thanks, Wally."

"Hey," he said. "Don't mention it. We gotta look out for each other, you know what I mean? Here in Gotham City."

THE MERCIFUL ANGEL OF DEATH

People come here to die, Mr. Scudder. They check out of
hospitals, give up their apartments, and come to Caritas.
Because they know we'll keep them comfortable here.
And they know we'll let them die."

Carl Orcott was long and lean, with a long sharp nose
and a matching chin. Some gray showed in his fair hair
and his strawberry-blond mustache. His facial skin was
stretched tight over his skull, and there were hollows in
his cheeks. He might have been naturally spare of flesh,
or worn down by the demands of his job. Because he
was a gay man in the last decade of a terrible century,
another possibility suggested itself. That he was HIV-
positive. That his immune system was compromised.
That the virus that would one day kill him was already
within him, waiting.

"Since an easy death is our whole reason for being,"
he was saying, "it seems a bit much to complain when it
occurs. Death is not the enemy here. Death is a friend.
Our people are in very bad shape by the time they come
to us. You don't run to a hospice when you get the initial

results from a blood test, or when the first purple K-S lesions show up. First you try everything, including denial, and everything works for a while, and finally nothing works, not the AZT, not the pentamidine, not the Louise Hay tapes, not the crystal healing. Not even the denial. When you're ready for it to be over, you come here and we see you out." He smiled thinly. "We hold the door for you. We don't boot you through it."

"But now you think — "

"I don't know what I think." He selected a briar pipe from a walnut stand that held eight of them, examined it, sniffed its bowl. "Grayson Lewes shouldn't have died," he said. "Not when he did. He was doing very well, relatively speaking. He was in agony, he had a CMV infection that was blinding him, but he was still strong. Of course he was dying, they're all dying, everybody's dying, but death certainly didn't appear to be imminent."

"What happened?"

"He died."

"What killed him?"

"I don't know." He breathed in the smell of the unlit pipe. "Someone went in and found him dead. There was no autopsy. There generally isn't. What would be the point? Doctors would just as soon not cut up AIDS patients anyway, not wanting the added risk of infection. Of course, most of our general staff are seropositive, but even so you try to avoid unnecessary additional exposure. Quantity could make a difference, and there could be multiple strains. The virus mutates, you see." He shook his head. "There's such a great deal we still don't know."

"There was no autopsy."

"No. I thought about ordering one."

"What stopped you?"

"The same thing that keeps people from getting the antibody test. Fear of what I might find."

"You think someone killed Lewes."

"I think it's possible."

"Because he died abruptly. But people do that, don't they? Even if they're not sick to begin with. They have strokes or heart attacks."

"That's true."

"This happened before, didn't it? Lewes wasn't the first."

He smiled ruefully. "You're good at this."

"It's what I do."

"Yes." His fingers were busy with the pipe. "There have been a few unexpected deaths. But there would be, as you've said. So there was no real cause for suspicion. There still isn't."

"But you're suspicious."

"Am I? I guess I am."

"Tell me the rest of it, Carl."

"I'm sorry," he said. "I'm making you drag it out of me, aren't I? Grayson Lewes had a visitor. She was in his room for twenty minutes, perhaps half an hour. She was the last person to see him alive. She may have been the first person to see him dead."

"Who is she?"

"I don't know. She's been coming here for months. She always brings flowers, something cheerful. She brought yellow freesias the last time. Nothing fancy, just a five-dollar bunch from the Korean on the corner, but they do brighten a room."

"Had she visited Lewes before?"

He shook his head. "Other people. Every week or so she would turn up, always asking for one of our residents by name. It's often the sickest of the sick that she comes to see."

"And then they die?"

"Not always. But often enough so that it's been remarked upon. Still, I never let myself think that she played a causative role. I thought she had some instinct that drew her to your side when you were circling the drain." He looked off to the side. "When she visited Lewes, someone joked that we'd probably have his room available soon. When you're on staff here, you become quite irreverent in private. Otherwise you'd go crazy."

"It was the same way on the police force."

"I'm not surprised. When one of us would cough or sneeze, another might say, 'Uh-oh, you might be in line for a visit from Mercy.' "

"Is that her name?"

"Nobody knows her name. It's what we call her among ourselves. The Merciful Angel of Death. Mercy, for short."

A man named Bobby sat up in bed in his fourth-floor room. He had short gray hair and a gray brush mustache and a gray complexion bruised purple here and there by Kaposi's Sarcoma. For all of the ravages of the disease, he had a heartbreakingly youthful face. He was a ruined cherub, the oldest boy in the world.

"She was here yesterday," he said.

"She visited you twice," Carl said.

"Twice?"

"Once last week and once three or four days ago."

"I thought it was one time. And I thought it was yesterday." He frowned. "It all seems like yesterday."

"What does, Bobby?"

"Everything. Camp Arrowhead. *I Love Lucy*. The moon shot. One enormous yesterday with everything crammed into it, like his closet. I don't remember his name but he was famous for his closet."

"Fibber McGee," Carl said.

"I don't know why I can't remember his name,"

Bobby said languidly. "It'll come to me. I'll think of it yesterday."

I said, "When she came to see you — "

"She was beautiful. Tall, slim, gorgeous eyes. A flowing dove-gray robe, a blood-red scarf at her throat. I wasn't sure if she was real or not. I thought she might be a vision."

"Did she tell you her name?"

"I don't remember. She said she was there to be with me. And mostly she just sat there, where Carl's sitting. She held my hand."

"What else did she say?"

"That I was safe. That no one could hurt me anymore. She said — "

"Yes?"

"That I was innocent," he said, and he sobbed and let his tears flow.

He wept freely for a few moments, then reached for a Kleenex. When he spoke again his voice was matter-of-fact, even detached. "She *was* here twice," he said. "I remember now. The second time I got snotty, I really had the rag on, and I told her she didn't have to hang around if she didn't want to. And she said *I* didn't have to hang around if I didn't want to.

"And I said, right, I can go tap-dancing down Broadway with a rose in my teeth. And she said, no, all I have to do is let go and my spirit will soar free. And I looked at her, and I knew what she meant."

"And?"

"She told me to let go, to give it all up, to just let go and go to the light. And I said — this is strange, you know?"

"What did you say, Bobby?"

"I said I couldn't see the light and I wasn't ready to go to it. And she said that was all right, that when I was ready the light would be there to guide me. She said I would know how to do it when the time came. And she talked about how to do it."

"How?"

"By letting go. By going to the light. I don't remember everything she said. I don't even know for sure if all of it happened, or if I dreamed part of it. I never know anymore. Sometimes I have dreams and later they feel like part of my personal history. And sometimes I look back at my life and most of it has a veil over it, as if I never lived it at all, as if it were nothing but a dream."

Back in his office Carl picked up another pipe and brought its blackened bowl to his nose. He said, "You asked why I called you instead of the police. Can you imagine putting Bobby through an official interrogation?"

"He seems to go in and out of lucidity."

He nodded. "The virus penetrates the blood-brain barrier. If you survive the K-S and the opportunistic infections, the reward is dementia. Bobby is mostly clear, but some of his mental circuits are beginning to burn out. Or rust out, or clog up, or whatever it is that they do."

"There are cops who know how to take testimony from people like that."

"Even so. Can you see the tabloid headlines? MERCY KILLER STRIKES AIDS HOSPICE. We have a hard enough time getting by as it is. You know, whenever the press happens to mention how many dogs and cats the SPCA puts to sleep, donations drop to a trickle. Imagine what would happen to us."

"Some people would give you more."

He laughed. " 'Here's a thousand dollars — kill ten of 'em for me.' You could be right."

He sniffed at the pipe again. I said, "You know, as

far as I'm concerned you can go ahead and smoke that thing."

He stared at me, then at the pipe, as if surprised to find it in his hand. "There's no smoking anywhere in the building," he said. "Anyway, I don't smoke."

"The pipes came with the office?"

He colored. "They were John's," he said. "We lived together. He died . . . God, it'll be two years in November. It doesn't seem that long."

"I'm sorry, Carl."

"I used to smoke cigarettes, Marlboros, but I quit ages ago. But I never minded his pipe smoke, though. I always liked the aroma. And now I'd rather smell one of his pipes than the AIDS smell. Do you know the smell I mean?"

"Yes."

"Not everyone with AIDS has it but a lot of them do, and most sickrooms reek of it. You must have smelled it in Bobby's room. It's an unholy musty smell, a smell like rotted leather. I can't stand the smell of leather anymore. I used to love leather, but now I can't help associating it with the stink of gay men wasting away in fetid airless rooms.

"And this whole building smells that way to me. There's the stench of disinfectant over everything. We use tons of it, spray and liquid. The virus is surprisingly frail, it doesn't last long outside the body, but we leave as little as possible to chance, and so the rooms and halls all smell of disinfectant. But underneath it, always, there's the smell of the disease itself."

He turned the pipe over in his hands. "His clothes were full of the smell. John's. I gave everything away. But his pipes held a scent I had always associated with him, and a pipe is such a personal thing, isn't it, with the smoker's toothmarks in the stem." He looked at me. His eyes were dry, his voice strong and steady. There was no grief in his tone, only in the words themselves. "Two years in November, though I swear it doesn't seem that long, and I use one smell to keep another at bay. And, I suppose, to bridge the gap of years, to keep him a little closer to me." He put the pipe down. "Back to cases. Will you take a careful but unofficial look at our Angel of Death?"

I said I would. He said I'd want a retainer, and opened the top drawer of his desk. I told him it wouldn't be necessary.

"But isn't that standard for private detectives?"

"I'm not one, not officially. I don't have a license."

"So you told me, but even so — "

"I'm not a lawyer, either," I went on, "but there's no reason why I can't do a little *pro bono* work once in a while. If it takes too much of my time I'll let you know, but for now let's call it a donation."

The hospice was in the Village, on Hudson Street. Rachel Bookspan lived five miles north in an Italianate brownstone on Claremont Avenue. Her husband, Paul, walked to work at Columbia University, where he was an associate professor of political science. Rachel was a free-lance copy editor, hired by several publishers to prepare manuscripts for publication. Her specialties were history and biography.

She told me all this over coffee in her book-lined living room. She talked about a manuscript she was working on, the biography of a woman who had founded a religious sect in the late nineteenth century. She talked about her children, two boys, who would be home from school in an hour or so. Finally she ran out of steam and I brought the conversation back to her brother, Arthur Fineberg, who had lived on Morton Street and worked downtown as a librarian for an investment firm. And who had died two weeks ago at the Caritas Hospice.

"How we cling to life," she said. "Even when it's awful. Even when we yearn for death."

"Did your brother want to die?"

"He prayed for it. Every day the disease took a little more from him, gnawing at him like a mouse, and after months and months and months of hell it finally took his will to live. He couldn't fight anymore. He had nothing to fight with, nothing to fight *for*. But he went on living all the same."

She looked at me, then looked away. "He begged me to kill him," she said.

I didn't say anything.

"How could I refuse him? But how could I help him? First I thought it wasn't right, but then I decided it was his life, and who had a better right to end it if he wanted to? But how could I do it? How?

"I thought of pills. We don't have anything in the house except Midol for cramps. I went to my doctor and said I had trouble sleeping. Well, that was true enough. He gave me a prescription for a dozen Valium. I didn't even bother getting it filled. I didn't want to give Artie a handful of tranquilizers. I wanted to give him one of those cyanide capsules the spies always had in World War Two movies. You bite down and you're gone. But where do you go to get something like that?"

She sat forward in her chair. "Do you remember that man in the Midwest who unhooked his kid from a respirator? The doctors wouldn't let the boy die and the father went into the hospital with a gun and held everybody at bay until his son was dead. I think that man was a hero."

"A lot of people thought so."

"God, I wanted to be a hero! I had fantasies. There's a Robinson Jeffers poem about a crippled hawk and the narrator puts it out of its misery. 'I gave him the lead gift,' he says. Meaning a bullet, a gift of lead. I wanted to give my brother that gift. I don't have a gun. I don't even believe in guns. At least I never did. I don't know what I believe in anymore.

"If I'd had a gun, could I have gone in there and shot him? I don't see how. I have a knife, I have a kitchen full of knives, and believe me, I thought of going in there with a knife in my purse and waiting until he dozed off and then slipping the knife between his ribs and into his heart. I visualized it, I went over every aspect of it, but I didn't do it. My God, I never even left the house with a knife in my bag."

She asked if I wanted more coffee. I said I didn't. I asked her if her brother had had other visitors, and if he might have made the same request of one of them.

"He had dozens of friends, men and women who loved him. And yes, he would have asked them. He told everybody he wanted to die. As hard as he fought to live, for all those months, that's how determined he became to die. Do you think someone helped him?"

"I think it's possible."

"God, I hope so," she said. "I just wish it had been me."

"I haven't had the test," Aldo said. "I'm a forty-four-year-old gay man who led an active sex life since I was fifteen. I don't *have* to take the test, Matthew. I assume I'm seropositive. I assume everybody is."

He was a plump teddy bear of a man, with curly black hair and a face as permanently buoyant as a smile button. We were sharing a small table at a coffeehouse on Bleecker, just two doors from the shop where he sold comic books and baseball cards to collectors.

"I may not develop the disease," he said. "I may die a perfectly respectable death due to overindulgence in food and drink. I may get hit by a bus or struck down by a mugger. If I do get sick I'll wait until it gets really bad, because I love this life, Matthew, I really do. But when the time comes I don't want to make local stops. I'm gonna catch an express train out of here."

"You sound like a man with his bags packed."

"No luggage. Travelin' light. You remember the song?"

"Of course."

He hummed a few bars of it, his foot tapping out the rhythm, our little marble-topped table shaking with the motion. He said, "I have pills enough to do the job. I also have a loaded handgun. And I think I have the nerve to do what I have to do, when I have to do it." He frowned, an uncharacteristic expression for him. "The danger lies in waiting too long. Winding up in a hospital bed too weak to do anything, too addled by brain fever to remember what it was you were supposed to do. Wanting to die but unable to manage it."

"I've heard there are people who'll help."

"You've heard that, have you?"

"One woman in particular."

"What are you after, Matthew?"

"You were a friend of Grayson Lewes. And of Arthur Fineberg. There's a woman who helps people who want to die. She may have helped them."

"And?"

"And you know how to get in touch with her."

"Who says?"

"I forget, Aldo."

The smile was back. "You're discreet, huh?"

"Very."

"I don't want to make trouble for her."

"Neither do I."

"Then why not leave her alone?"

"There's a hospice administrator who's afraid she's murdering people. He called me in rather than start an official police inquiry. But if I don't get anywhere — "

"He calls the cops." He found his address book, copied out a number for me. "Please don't make trouble for her," he said. "I might need her myself."

I called her that evening, met her the following afternoon at a cocktail lounge just off Washington Square. She was as described, even to the gray cape over a long gray dress. Her scarf today was canary yellow. She was drinking Perrier, and I ordered the same.

She said, "Tell me about your friend. You say he's very ill."

"He wants to die. He's been begging me to kill him but I can't do it."

"No, of course not."

"I was hoping you might be able to visit him."

"If you think it might help. Tell me something about him, why don't you."

I don't suppose she was more than forty-five, if that, but there was something ancient about her face. You didn't need much of a commitment to reincarnation to believe she had lived before. Her facial features were pronounced, her eyes a graying blue. Her voice was pitched low, and along with her height it raised doubts about her sexuality. She might have been a sex change, or a drag queen. But I didn't think so. There was an Eternal Female quality to her that didn't feel like parody.

I said, "I can't."

"Because there's no such person."

"I'm afraid there are plenty of them, but I don't have one in mind." I told her in a couple of sentences why I was there. When I'd finished she let the silence stretch, then asked me if I thought she could kill anyone. I told her it was hard to know what anyone could do.

She said, "I think you should see for yourself what it is that I do."

She stood up. I put some money on the table and followed her out to the street.

We took a cab to a four-story brick building on Twenty-second Street west of Ninth. We climbed two flights of stairs, and the door opened when she knocked on it. I could smell the disease before I was across the threshold. The young black man who opened the door was glad to see her and unsurprised by my presence. He didn't ask my name or tell me his.

"Kevin's so tired," he told us both. "It breaks my heart."

We walked through a neat, sparsely furnished living room and down a short hallway to a bedroom, where the smell was stronger. Kevin lay in a bed with its head cranked up. He looked like a famine victim, or someone liberated from Dachau. Terror filled his eyes.

She pulled a chair up to the side of his bed and sat in it. She took his hand in hers and used her free hand to stroke his forehead. "You're safe now," she told him. "You're safe, you don't have to hurt anymore, you did all the things you had to do. You can relax now, you can let go now, you can go to the light.

"You can do it," she told him. "Close your eyes, Kevin, and go inside yourself and find the part that's holding on. Somewhere within you there's a part of you that's like a clenched fist, and I want you to find that part and be with that part. And let go. Let the fist open its fingers. It's as if the fist is holding a little bird, and if you open up the hand the bird can fly free. Just let it happen, Kevin. Just let go."

He was straining to talk, but the best he could do was make a sort of cawing sound. She turned to the black man, who was standing in the doorway. "David," she said, "his parents aren't living, are they?"

"I believe they're both gone."

"Which one was he closest to?"

"I don't know. I believe they're both gone a long time now."

"Did he have a lover? Before you, I mean."

"Kevin and I were never lovers. I don't even know him that well. I'm here 'cause he hasn't got anybody else. He had a lover."

"Did his lover die? What was his name?"

"Martin."

"Kevin," she said, "you're going to be all right now. All you have to do is go to the light. Do you see the light? Your mother's there, Kevin, and your father, and Martin — "

"Mark!" David cried. "Oh, God, I'm sorry, I'm so stupid, it wasn't Martin, it was Mark, Mark, that was his name."

"That's all right, David."

"I'm so damn stupid — "

"Look into the light, Kevin," she said. "Mark is there, and your parents, and everyone who ever loved you. Matthew, take his other hand. Kevin, you don't have to stay here anymore, darling. You did everything you came here to do. You don't have to stay. You don't have to hold on. You can let go, Kevin. You can go to the light. Let go and reach out to the light — "

I don't know how long she talked to him. Fifteen, twenty minutes, I suppose. Several times he made the cawing sound, but for the most part he was silent.

Nothing seemed to be happening, and then I realized that his terror was no longer a presence. She seemed to have talked it away. She went on talking to him, stroking his brow and holding his hand, and I held his other hand. I was no longer listening to what she was saying, just letting the words wash over me while my mind played with some tangled thought like a kitten with yarn.

Then something happened. The energy in the room shifted and I looked up, knowing that he was gone.

"Yes," she murmured. "Yes, Kevin. God bless you, God give you rest. Yes."

"Sometimes they're stuck," she said. "They want to go but they can't. They've been hanging on so long, you see, that they don't know how to stop."

"So you help them."

"If I can."

"What if you can't? Suppose you talk and talk and they still hold on?"

"Then they're not ready. They'll be ready another time. Sooner or later everybody lets go, everybody dies. With or without my help."

"And when they're not ready — "

"Sometimes I come back another time. And sometimes they're ready then."

"What about the ones who beg for help? The ones like Arthur Fineberg, who plead for death but aren't physically close enough to it to let go?"

"What do you want me to say?"

"The thing you want to say. The thing that's stuck in your throat, the way his own unwanted life was stuck in Kevin's throat. You're holding on to it."

"Just let it go, eh?"

"If you want."

We were walking somewhere in Chelsea, and we walked a full block now without either of us saying a word. Then she said, "I think there's a world of difference between assisting someone verbally and doing anything physical to hasten death."

"So do I."

"And that's where I draw the line. But sometimes, having drawn that line — "

"You step over it."

"Yes. The first time I swear I acted without conscious intent. I used a pillow, I held it over his face and — " She breathed deeply. "I swore it would never happen again. But then there was someone else, and he just needed help, you know, and — "

"And you helped him."

"Yes. Was I wrong?"

"I don't know what's right or wrong."

"Suffering is wrong," she said, "unless it's part of His plan, and how can I presume to decide if it is or not? Maybe people can't let go because there's one more lesson they have to learn before they move on. Who the hell am I to decide it's time for somebody's life to end? How dare I interfere?"

"And yet you do."

"Just once in a while, when I just don't see a way around it. Then I do what I have to do. I'm sure I must have a choice in the matter, but I swear it doesn't feel that way. It doesn't feel as though I have any choice at all." She stopped walking, turned to look at me. She said, "Now what happens?"

"Well, she's the Merciful Angel of Death," I told Carl Orcott. "She visits the sick and dying, almost always at somebody's invitation. A friend contacts her, or a relative."

"Do they pay her?"

"Sometimes they try to. She won't take any money. She even pays for the flowers herself." She'd taken Dutch iris to Kevin's apartment on Twenty-second Street. Blue, with yellow centers that matched her scarf.

"She does it *pro bono*," he said.

"And she talks to them. You heard what Bobby said. I got to see her in action. She talked the poor son of a bitch straight out of this world and into the next one. I suppose you could argue that what she does comes perilously close to hypnosis, that she hypnotizes people and convinces them to kill themselves psychically, but I can't imagine anybody trying to sell that to a jury."

"She just talks to them."

"Uh-huh. 'Let go, go to the light.' "

" 'And have a nice day.' "

"That's the idea."

"She's not killing people?"

"Nope. Just letting them die."

He picked up a pipe. "Well, hell," he said, "that's what we do. Maybe I ought to put her on staff." He sniffed the pipe bowl. "You have my thanks, Matthew. Are you sure you don't want some of our money to go with it? Just because Mercy works *pro bono* doesn't mean you should have to."

"That's all right."

"You're certain?"

I said, "You asked me the first day if I knew what AIDS smelled like."

"And you said you'd smelled it before. Oh."

I nodded. "I've lost friends to it. I'll lose more before it's over. In the meantime I'm grateful when I get the chance to do you a favor. Because I'm glad this place is here, so people have a place to come to."

Even I was glad she was around, the woman in gray, the Merciful Angel of Death. To hold the door for them, and show them the light on the other side. And, if they really needed it, to give them the least little push through it.

THE NIGHT AND THE MUSIC

We left halfway through the curtain calls, threading our way up the aisle and across the lobby. Inside it had been winter in Paris, with *La Bohème*'s lovers shivering and starving; outside it was New York, with spring turning into summer.

We held hands and walked across the great courtyard, past the fountain shimmering under the lights, past Avery Fisher Hall. Our apartment is in the Parc Vendome, at Fifty-seventh and Ninth, and we headed in that direction and walked a block or so in silence.

Then Elaine said, "I don't want to go home."

"All right."

"I want to hear music. Can we do that?"

"We just did that."

"Different music. Not another opera."

"Good," I said, "because one a night is my limit."

"You old bear. One a night is one over your limit."

I shrugged. "I'm learning to like it."

"Well, one a night's my limit. You know something? I'm in a mood."

"Somehow I sensed as much."

"She always dies," she said.

"Mimi."

"Uh-huh. How many times do you suppose I've seen *La Bohème*? Six, seven times?"

"If you say so."

"At least. You know what? I could see it a hundred times and it's not going to change. She'll die every fucking time. "

"Odds are."

"So I want to hear something different," she said, "before we call it a night."

"Something happy," I suggested.

"No, sad is fine. I don't mind sad. As a matter of fact I prefer it."

"But you want them all alive at the end."

"That's it," she said. "Sad as can be, so long as nobody dies."

We caught a cab to a new place I'd heard about on the ground floor of a high-rise on Amsterdam in the Nineties. The crowd was salt and pepper, white college kids and black strivers, blonde fashion models and black players. The group was mixed, too; the tenor man and the bass player were white, the pianist and the drummer black. The *maître d'* thought he recognized me and put us at a table near the bandstand. They were a few bars into "Satin Doll" when we sat down and they followed it with a tune I recognized but couldn't name. I think it was a Thelonious Monk composition, but that's just a guess. I can hardly ever name the tune unless there's a lyric to it that sticks in my mind.

Aside from ordering drinks, we didn't say a word until the set ended. We sipped our cranberry juice and soda and listened to the music. She watched the musicians and I watched her watch them. When they took a break she reached for my hand. "Thanks," she said.

"You okay?"

"I was always okay. I do feel better now, though. You know what I was thinking?"

"The night we met."

Her eyes widened. "How'd you know that?"

"Well, it was in a room that looked and felt a lot like this one. You were at Danny Boy's table, and this is his kind of place."

"God, I was young. We were both so goddamned young."

"Youth is one of those things time cures."

"You were a cop and I was a hooker. But you'd been on the force longer than I'd been on the game."

"I already had a gold shield."

"And I was new enough to think the life was glamorous. Well, it *was* glamorous. Look at the places I went and the people I got to meet."

"Married cops."

"That's right, you were married then."

"I'm married now."

"To me. Jesus, the way things turn out, huh?"

"A club like this," I said, "and the same kind of music playing."

"Sad enough to break your heart, but nobody dies."

"You were the most beautiful woman in the room that night," I said. "And you still are."

"Ah, Pinocchio," she said, and squeezed my hand. "Lie to me."

We closed the place. Outside on the street she said, "God, I'm impossible. I don't want the night to end."

"It doesn't have to."

"In the old days," she said, "you knew all the after-hours joints. Remember when Condon's would stay open late for musicians, and they'd jam until dawn?"

"I remember Eddie Condon's hangover cure," I said. "'Take the juice of two quarts of whiskey . . .' I forget what came after that."

"Oblivion?"

"You'd think so. Say, I know where we can go."

I flagged a cab and we rode down to Sheridan Square, where there's a basement joint with the same name as a long-gone Harlem jazz club. They start around midnight and stay open past dawn, and it's legal because they don't serve alcohol. I used to go to late joints for the booze, and I learned to like the music because I heard so much of it there, and because you could just about taste the alcohol in every flatted fifth. Nowadays I go for the music, and what I hear in the blue notes is not so much the booze as all the feelings the drink used to mask.

That night there were a lot of different musicians sitting in with what I guess was the house rhythm section. There was a tenor player who sounded a little like Johnny Griffin and a piano player who reminded me of Lennie Tristano. And as always there was a lot of music I barely heard, background music for my own unfocused thoughts.

The sky was light by the time we dragged ourselves out of there. "Look at that," Elaine said. "It's bright as day."

"And well it might be. It's morning."

"What a New York night, huh? You know, I loved our trip to Europe, and other places we've gone together, but when you come right down to it — "

"You're a New York kind of gal."

"You bet your ass. And what we heard tonight was New York music. I know all about the music coming up the river from New Orleans, all that crap, and I don't care. That was New York music."

"You're right."

"And nobody died," she said.

"That's right," I said. "Nobody died."

LOOKING FOR DAVID

Elaine said, "You never stop working, do you?"

I looked at her. We were in Florence, sitting at a little tile-topped table in the Piazza di San Marco, sipping cappuccino every bit as good as the stuff they served at the Peacock on Greenwich Avenue. It was a bright day but the air was cool and crisp, the city bathed in October light. Elaine was wearing khakis and a tailored safari jacket, and looked like a glamorous foreign correspondent, or perhaps a spy. I was wearing khakis, too, and a polo shirt, and the blue blazer she called my Old Reliable.

We'd had five days in Venice. This was the second of five days in Florence, and then we'd have six days in Rome before Alitalia took us back home again.

I said, "Nice work if you can get it."

"Uh-uh," she said. "I caught you. You were scanning the area the way you always do."

"I was a cop for a lot of years."

"I know, and I guess it's a habit a person doesn't

outgrow. And not a bad one, either. I have some New York street smarts myself, but I can't send my eyes around a room and pick up what you can. And you don't even think about it. You do it automatically."

"I guess. But I wouldn't call it working."

"When we're supposed to be basking in the beauties of Florence," she said, "and exclaiming over the classic beauty of the sculpture in the piazza, and instead you're staring at an old queen in a white linen jacket five tables over, trying to guess if he's got a yellow sheet and just what's written on it — wouldn't you call that working?"

"There's no guesswork required," I said. "I know what it says on his yellow sheet."

"You do?"

"His name is Horton Pollard," I said. "If it's the same man, and if I've been sending a lot of looks his way it's to make sure he's the man I think he is. It's well over twenty years since I've seen him. Probably more like twenty-five." I glanced over and watched the white-haired gentleman saying something to the waiter. He raised an eyebrow in a manner that was at once arrogant and apologetic. It was as good as a fingerprint. "It's him," I said. "Horton Pollard. I'm positive."

"Why don't you go over and say hello?"

"He might not want that."

"Twenty-five years ago you were still on the job. What did you do, arrest him?"

"Uh-huh."

"Honestly? What did *he* do? Art fraud? That's what comes to mind, sitting at an outdoor table in Florence, but he was probably just a stock swindler."

"Something white-collar, in other words."

"Something flowing-collar, from the looks of him. I give up. What did he do?"

I'd been looking his way, and our glances caught. I saw recognition come into his eyes, and his eyebrows went up again in that manner that was unmistakably his. He pushed his chair back, got to his feet.

"Here he comes," I said. "You can ask him yourself."

"Mr. Scudder," he said. "I want to say Martin, but I know that's not right. Help me out."

"Matthew, Mr. Pollard. And this is my wife, Elaine."

"How fortunate for you," he told me, and took the hand she extended. "I looked over here and thought, What a beautiful woman! Then I looked again and thought, I know that fellow. But then it took me a minute to place you. The name came first, or the surname, at any rate. His name's Scudder, but how do I know him? And then of course the rest of it came to me, all but your first name. I knew it wasn't Martin, but I couldn't sweep that name out of my mind and let Matthew come in." He sighed. "It's a curious muscle, the memory. Or aren't you old enough yet to have found it so?"

"My memory's still pretty good."

"Oh, mine's *good*," he said. "It's just capricious. Willful, I sometimes think."

At my invitation, he pulled up a chair from a nearby table and sat down. "But only for a moment," he said, and asked what brought us to Italy, and how long we'd be in Florence. He lived here, he told us. He'd lived here for quite a few years now. He knew our hotel, on the east bank of the Arno, and pronounced it charming and a good value. He mentioned a café just down the street from the hotel that we really ought to try.

"Although you certainly don't need to follow my

recommendations," he said, "or Michelin's, either. You can't get a bad meal in Florence. Well, that's not *entirely* true. If you insist on going to high-priced restaurants, you'll encounter the occasional disappointment. But if you simply blunder into whatever humble trattoria is closest, you'll dine well every time."

"I think we've been dining a little too well," Elaine said.

"It's a danger," he acknowledged, "although the Florentines manage to stay quite slim themselves. I started to bulk up a bit when I first came here. How could one help it? Everything tasted so good. But I took off the pounds I gained and I've kept them off. Though I sometimes wonder why I bother. For God's sake, I'm seventy-six years old."

"You don't look it," she told him.

"I wouldn't care to look it. But why is that, do you suppose? No one else on God's earth gives a damn what I look like. Why should it matter to me?"

She said it was self-respect, and he mused on the difficulty of telling where self-respect left off and vanity began. Then he said he was staying too long at the fair, wasn't he, and got to his feet. "But you must visit me," he said. "My villa is not terribly grand, but it's quite nice and I'm proud enough of it to want to show it off. Please tell me you'll come for lunch tomorrow."

"Well . . ."

"It's settled, then," he said, and gave me his card. "Any cabdriver will know how to find it. Set the price in advance, though. Some of them will cheat you, although most are surprisingly honest. Shall we say one o'clock?" He leaned forward, placed his palms on the table. "I've thought of you often over the years, Matthew. Especially here, sipping *caffè nero* a few yards from Michelangelo's

David. It's not the original, you know. That's in a museum, though even the museums are less than safe these days. You know the Uffizzi was bombed a few years ago?"

"I read about that."

"The Mafia. Back home they just kill each other. Here they blow up masterpieces. Still, it's a wonderfully civilized country, by and large. And I suppose I had to wind up here, near the David." He'd lost me, and I guess he knew it, because he frowned, annoyed at himself. "I just ramble," he said. "I suppose the one thing I'm short of here is people to talk to. And I always thought I could talk to you, Matthew. Circumstances prevented my so doing, of course, but over the years I regretted the lost opportunity." He straightened up. "Tomorrow, one o'clock. I look forward to it."

Well, of course I'm dying to go," Elaine said. "I'd love to see what his place looks like. 'It's not terribly grand but it's quite nice.' I'll bet it's nice. I'll bet it's gorgeous."

"You'll find out tomorrow."

"I don't know. He wants to talk to you, and three might be a crowd for the kind of conversation he wants to have. It wasn't art theft you arrested him for, was it?"

"No."

"Did he kill someone?"

"His lover."

"Well, that's what each man does, isn't it? Kills the thing he loves, according to what'shisname."

"Oscar Wilde."

"Thanks, Mr. Memory. Actually, I knew that. Sometimes when a person says what'shisname or whatchamacallit it's not because she can't remember. It's just a conversational device."

"I see."

She gave me a searching look. "There was something about it," she said. "What?"

"It was brutal." My mind filled with a picture of the murder scene, and I blinked it away. "You see a lot on the job, and most of it's ugly, but this was pretty bad."

"He seems so gentle. I'd expect any murder he committed to be virtually nonviolent."

"There aren't many non-violent murders."

"Well, bloodless, anyway."

"This was anything but."

"Well, don't keep me in suspense. What did he do?"

"He used a knife," I said.

"And stabbed him?"

"Carved him," I said. "His lover was younger than Pollard, and I guess he was a good-looking man, but you couldn't prove it by me. What I saw looked like what's left of the turkey the day after Thanksgiving."

"Well, that's vivid enough," she said. "I have to say I get the picture."

"I was first on the scene except for the two uniforms who caught the squeal, and they were young enough to strike a cynical pose."

"While you were old enough not to. Did you throw up?"

"No, after a few years you just don't. But it was as bad as anything I'd ever seen."

Horton Pollard's villa was north of the city, and if it wasn't grand it was nevertheless beautiful, a white stuccoed gem set on a hillside with a commanding view of the valley. He showed us through the rooms, answered Elaine's questions about the paintings and furnishings, and accepted her explanation of why she couldn't stay for lunch. Or appeared to — as she rode off in the taxi that had brought us, something in his expression suggested for an instant that he felt slighted by her departure

"We'll dine on the terrace," he said. "But what's the matter with me? I haven't offered you a drink. What will you have, Matthew? The bar's well stocked, although I don't know that Paolo has a very extensive repertoire of cocktails."

I said that any kind of sparkling water would be fine. He said something in Italian to his house boy, then gave me an appraising glance and asked me if I would want wine with our lunch.

I said I wouldn't. "I'm glad I thought to ask," he said. "I was going to open a bottle and let it breathe, but now it can just go on holding its breath. You used to drink, if I remember correctly."

"Yes, I did."

"The night it all happened," he said. "It seems to me you told me I looked as though I needed a drink. And I got out a bottle, and you poured drinks for both of us. I remember being surprised you were allowed to drink on duty."

"I wasn't," I said, "but I didn't always let that stop me."

"And now you don't drink at all?"

"I don't, but that's no reason why you shouldn't have wine with lunch."

"But I never do," he said. "I couldn't while I was locked up, and when I was released I found I didn't care for it, the taste or the physical sensation. I drank the odd glass of wine anyway, for a while, because I thought one couldn't be entirely civilized without it. Then I realized I didn't care. That's quite the nicest thing about age, perhaps the only good thing to be said for it. Increasingly, one ceases to care about more and more things, particularly the opinions of others. Different for you, though, wasn't it? You stopped because you had to."

"Yes."

"Do you miss it?"

"Now and then."

"I don't, but then I was never that fond of it. There was a time when I could distinguish different châteaux in a blind tasting, but the truth of the matter was that I never cared for any of them all that much, and after-dinner cognac gave me heartburn. And now I drink mineral water with my meals, and coffee after them. *Acqua minerale.* There's a favorite trattoria of mine where the owner calls it *acqua miserabile.* But he'd as soon sell me it as anything else. He doesn't care, and *I* shouldn't care if he did."

Lunch was simple but elegant — a green salad, ravioli with butter and sage, and a nice piece of fish. Our conversation was mostly about Italy, and I was sorry Elaine hadn't stayed to hear it. He had a lot to say — about the way art permeated everyday Florentine life, about the longstanding enthusiasm of the British upper classes for the city — and I found it absorbing enough, but it would have held more interest for her than for me.

Afterward Paolo cleared our dishes and served espresso. We fell silent, and I sipped my coffee and looked out at the view of the valley and wondered how long it would take for the eye to tire of it.

"I thought I would grow accustomed to it," he said, reading my mind. "But I haven't yet, and I don't think I ever will."

"How long have you been here?"

"Almost fifteen years. I came on a visit as soon as I could after my release."

"And you've never been back?"

He shook his head. "I came intending to stay, and once here I managed to arrange the necessary resident visa. It's not difficult if there's money, and I was fortunate. There's still plenty of money, and there always will be. I live well, but not terribly high. Even if I live longer than anyone should, there will be money sufficient to see me out."

"That makes it easier."

"It does," he agreed. "It didn't make the years inside any easier, I have to say that, but if I hadn't had money I might have spent them someplace even worse. Not that the place they put me was a pleasure dome."

"I suppose you were at a mental hospital."

"A facility for the criminally insane," he said, pronouncing the words precisely. "The phrase has a ring to it, doesn't it? And yet it was entirely appropriate. The act I performed was unquestionably criminal, and altogether insane."

He helped himself to more espresso. "I brought you here so that I could talk about it," he said. "Selfish of me, but that's part of being old. One becomes more selfish, or perhaps less concerned about concealing one's selfishness from oneself and others." He sighed. "One also becomes more direct, but in this instance it's hard to know where to start."

"Wherever you want," I suggested.

"With David, I suppose. Not the statue, though. The man."

"Maybe my memory's not all I like to think it is," I said. "Was your lover's name David? Because I could have sworn it was Robert. Robert Naismith, and there was a middle name, but that wasn't David, either."

"It was Paul," he said. "His name was Robert Paul Naismith. He wanted to be called Rob. I called him

David sometimes, but he didn't care for that. In my mind, though, he would always be David."

I didn't say anything. A fly buzzed in a corner, then went still. The silence stretched.

Then he began to talk.

"I grew up in Buffalo," he said. "I don't know if you've ever been there. A very beautiful city, at least in its nicer sections. Wide streets lined with elms. Some fine public buildings, some notable private homes. Of course the elms are all lost to Dutch Elm disease, and the mansions on Delaware Avenue now house law firms and dental clinics, but everything changes, doesn't it? I've come round to the belief that it's supposed to, but that doesn't mean one has to like it.

"Buffalo hosted the Pan-American Exposition, which was even before my time. It was held in 1901, if I remember correctly, and several of the buildings raised for the occasion remain to this day. One of the nicest, built alongside the city's principal park, has long been the home of the Buffalo Historical Society, and houses their museum collection.

"Are you wondering where this is leading? There was, and doubtless still is, a circular drive at the Historical Building's front, and in the midst of it stood a bronze copy of Michelangelo's David. It might conceivably be a casting, though I think we can safely assume it to be just a copy. It's life-size, at any rate — or I should say actual size, as Michelangelo's statue is itself considerably larger than life, unless the young David was built more along the lines of his adversary Goliath.

"You saw the statue yesterday — although, as I said, that too was a copy. I don't know how much attention you paid to it, but I wonder if you know what the sculptor is supposed to have said when asked how he managed to create such a masterpiece. It's such a wonderful line it would almost have to be apocryphal.

" 'I looked at the marble,' Michelangelo is said to have said, 'and I cut away the part that wasn't David.' That's almost as delicious as the young Mozart explaining that musical composition is the easiest thing in the world, you have merely to write down the music you hear in your head. Who cares, really, if either of them ever said any such thing? If they didn't, well, they ought to have done, wouldn't you say?

"I've known that statue all my life. I can't recall when I first saw it, but it must have been on my first visit to the Historical Building, and that would have been at a very early age. Our house was on Nottingham Terrace, not a ten-minute walk from the Historical Building, and I went there innumerable times as a boy. And it seems to me I always responded to the David. The stance, the attitude, the uncanny combination of strength and vulnerability, of fragility and confidence. And, of course, the sheer physical beauty of the David, the sexuality — but it was a while before I was aware of that aspect of it, or before I let myself acknowledge my awareness.

"When we all turned sixteen and got driver's licenses, David took on new meaning in our lives. The circular drive, you see, was the lovers' lane of choice for young couples who needed privacy. It was a pleasant parklike setting in a good part of town, unlike the few available alternatives in nasty neighborhoods down by the waterfront. Consequently, 'going to see David' became a euphemism for parking and making out — which, now that I think of it, are euphemisms themselves, aren't they?

"I saw a lot of David in my late teens. The irony, of course, is that I was far more drawn to his young masculine form than to the generous curves of the young women who were my companions on those visits. I was gay, it seems to me, from birth, but I didn't let myself know that. At first I denied the impulses. Later, when I learned to act on them — in Front Park, in the men's room at the Greyhound station — I denied that they meant anything. It was, I assured myself, a stage I was going through."

He pursed his lips, shook his head, sighed. "A lengthy stage," he said, "as I seem still to be going through it. I was aided in my denial by the fact that whatever I did with other young men was just an adjunct to my real life, which was manifestly normal. I went off to a good school, I came home at Christmas and during the summer, and wherever I was I enjoyed the company of women.

"Lovemaking in those years was usually a rather incomplete affair. Girls made a real effort to remain virginal, at least in a strictly technical sense, if not until marriage then until they were in what we nowadays call a committed relationship. I don't remember what we called it then, but I suspect it was a somewhat less cumbersome phrase.

"Still, sometimes one went all the way, and on those occasions I acquitted myself well enough. None of my partners had cause to complain. I could do it, you see, and I enjoyed it, and if it was less thrilling than what I found with male partners, well, chalk it up to the lure of the forbidden. It didn't have to mean there was anything *wrong* with me. It didn't mean I was *different* in any fundamental way.

"I led a normal life, Matthew. I would say I was determined to lead a normal life, but it never seemed to require much in the way of determination. During my senior year at college I became engaged to a girl I'd known literally all my life. Our parents were friends and we'd grown up together. I graduated and we were married. I took an advanced degree. My field was art history, as you may remember, and I managed to get an appointment to the faculty of the University of Buffalo. SUNY Buffalo, they call it now, but that was years before it became a part of the state university. It was just plain UB, with most of its student body drawn from the city and environs.

"We lived at first in an apartment near the campus, but then both sets of parents ponied up and we moved to a small house on Hallam, just about equidistant between the houses each of us had grown up in.

"It wasn't far from the statue of David, either."

He led a normal life, he explained. Fathered two children. Took up golf and joined the country club. He came into some family money, and a textbook he authored brought in royalties that grew more substantial each year. As the years passed, it became increasingly easy to believe that his relations with other men had indeed been a stage, and one he had essentially outgrown.

"I still felt things," he said, "but the need to act on them seemed to have passed. I might be struck by the physical appearance of one of my students, say, but I'd never do anything about it, or even seriously consider doing anything about it. I told myself my admiration was aesthetic, a natural response to male beauty. In youth, hormone-driven as one is, I'd confused this with actual sexual desire. Now I could recognize it for the innocent and asexual phenomenon it was."

Which was not to say that he'd given up his little adventures entirely.

"I would be invited somewhere to attend a conference," he said, "or to give a guest lecture. I'd be in another city where I didn't know anyone and nobody knew me. And I would have had a few drinks, and I'd feel the urge for some excitement. And I could tell myself that, while a liaison with another woman would be a betrayal of my wife and a violation of my marital vows, the same could hardly be said for some innocent sport with another man. So I'd go to the sort of bar one goes to — they were never hard to find, even in those closeted days, even in provincial cities and college towns. And, once there, it was never hard to find someone."

He was silent for a moment, gazing off toward the horizon.

"Then I walked into a bar in Madison, Wisconsin," he said, "and there he was."

"Robert Paul Naismith."

"David," he said. "That's who *I* saw, that's the youth on whom my eyes fastened the instant I cleared the threshold. I can remember the moment, you see. I can see him now exactly as I saw him then. He was wearing a dark silk shirt and tan trousers and loafers without socks, which no one wore in those days. He was standing at the bar with a drink in his hand, and his physique and the way he stood, the stance, the attitude — he was Michelangelo's David. More than that, he was *my* David. He was my ideal, he was the object of a lifelong quest I hadn't even known I was on, and I drank him in with my eyes and I was lost."

"Just like that," I said.

"Oh, yes," he agreed. "Just like that."

He was silent, and I wondered if he was waiting for me to prompt him. I decided he was not. He seemed to be choosing to remain in the memory for a moment.

Then he said, "Quite simply, I had never been in love with anybody. I have come to believe that it is a form of insanity. Not to love, to care deeply for another. That seems to me to be quite sane, and even ennobling. I loved my parents, certainly, and in a somewhat different way I loved my wife.

"This was categorically different. This was obsessive.

This was preoccupation. It was the collector's passion: I must have this painting, this statue, this postage stamp. I must embrace it, I must own it utterly. It and it alone will complete me. It will change my own nature. It will make me worthwhile.

"It wasn't sex, not really. I won't say sex had nothing to do with it. I was attracted to David as I'd never been attracted to anyone before. But at the same time I felt less driven sexually than I had on occasion in the past. I wanted to possess David. If I could do that, if I could make him entirely mine, it scarcely mattered if I had sex with him."

He fell silent, and this time I decided he was waiting to be prompted. I said, "What happened?"

"I threw my life over," he said. "On some flimsy pretext or other I stayed on in Madison for a week after the conference ended. Then I flew with David to New York and bought an apartment, the top floor of a brownstone in Turtle Bay. And then I flew back to Buffalo, alone, and told my wife I was leaving her."

He lowered his eyes. "I didn't want to hurt her," he said, "but of course I hurt her badly and deeply. She was not completely surprised, I don't believe, to learn there was a man involved. She'd inferred that much about me over the years, and probably saw it as part of the package, the downside of having a husband with an aesthetic sensibility.

"But she thought I cared for her, and I made it very clear that I did not. She was a woman who had never hurt anyone, and I caused her a good deal of pain, and I regret that and always will. It seems to me a far blacker sin than the one I served time for.

"Enough. I left her and moved to New York. Of course I resigned my tenured professorship at UB. I had connections throughout the academic world, to be sure, and a decent if not glorious reputation, so I might have found something at Columbia or NYU. But the scandal I'd created made that less likely, and anyway I no longer gave a damn for teaching. I just wanted to live, and enjoy my life.

"There was money enough to make that possible. We lived well. Too well, really. Not wisely but too well. Good restaurants every night, fine wines with dinner. Season tickets to the opera and the ballet. Summers in the Pines. Winters in Barbados or Bali. Trips to London and Paris and Rome. And the company, in town or abroad, of other rich queens."

"And?"

"And it went on like that," he said. He folded his hands in his lap, and a little smile played on his lips. "It went on, and then one day I picked up a knife and killed him. You know that part, Matthew. It's where you came in."

"Yes."

"But you don't know why."

"No, that never came out. Or if it did I missed it."

He shook his head. "It never came out. I didn't offer a defense, and I certainly didn't provide an explanation. But can you guess?"

"Why you killed him? I have no idea."

"But you must have come to know some of the reasons people have for killing other people? Why don't you humor an old sinner and try to guess. Prove to me that my motive was not unique after all."

"The reasons that come to mind are the obvious ones," I said, "and that probably rules them out. Let me see. He was leaving you. He was unfaithful to you. He had fallen in love with someone else."

"He would never have left," he said. "He adored the life we led and knew he could never live half so well with someone else. He would never fall in love with anyone else any more than he could have fallen in love with me. David was in love with himself. And of course he was unfaithful, and had been from the beginning, but I had never expected him to be otherwise."

"You realized you'd thrown your life away on him," I said, "and hated him for it."

"I *had* thrown my life away, but I didn't regret it. I'd been living a lie, and what loss to toss it aside? While jetting off to Paris for a weekend, does one long for the gentle pleasures of a classroom in Buffalo? Some may, for all I know. I never did."

I was ready to quit, but he insisted I come up with a few more guesses. They were all off the mark.

He said, "Give up? All right, I'll tell you. He changed."

"He changed?"

"When I met him," he said, "my David was the most beautiful creature I had ever set eyes on, the absolute embodiment of my lifelong ideal. He was slender but muscular, vulnerable yet strong. He was — well, go back to the San Marco piazza and look at the statue. Michelangelo got it just right. That's what he looked like."

"And then what? He got older?"

He set his jaw. "Everyone gets older," he said, "except for the ones who die young. It's unfair, but there's nothing for it. David didn't merely age. He coarsened. He thickened. He ate too much and drank too much and stayed up too late and took too many drugs. He put on weight. He got bloated. He grew jowly, and got pouchy under his eyes. His muscles wasted beneath their coating of fat and his flesh sagged.

"It didn't happen overnight. But that's how I experienced it, because the process was well along before I let myself see it. Finally I couldn't help but see it.

"I couldn't bear to look at him. Before I had been

unable to take my eyes off him, and now I found myself averting my gaze. I felt betrayed. I fell in love with a Greek god, and watched as he turned into a Roman emperor."

"And you killed him for that?"

"I wasn't trying to kill him."

I looked at him.

"Oh, I suppose I was, really. I'd been drinking, we'd both been drinking, and we'd had an argument, and I was angry. I don't suppose I was too far gone to know that he'd be dead when I was done, and that I'd have killed him. But that wasn't the point."

"It wasn't?"

"He passed out," he said. "He was lying there, naked, reeking of the wine seeping out of his pores, this great expanse of bloated flesh as white as marble. I suppose I hated him for having thus transformed himself, and I know I hated myself for having been an agent of his transformation. And I decided to do something about it."

He shook his head, and sighed deeply. "I went into the kitchen," he said, "and I came back with a knife. And I thought of the boy I'd seen that first night in Madison, and I thought of Michelangelo. And I tried to be Michelangelo."

I must have looked puzzled. He said, "Don't you remember? I took the knife and cut away the part that wasn't David."

It was a few days later in Rome when I recounted all this to Elaine. We were at an outdoor cafe near the Spanish Steps. "All those years," I said, "I took it for granted he was trying to destroy his lover. That's what mutilation generally is, the expression of a desire to annihilate.

But he wasn't trying to disfigure him, he was trying to *re*figure him."

"He was just a few years ahead of his time," she said. "Now they call it liposuction and charge the earth for it. I'll tell you one thing. As soon as we get back I'm going straight from the airport to the gym, before all this pasta becomes a permanent part of me. I'm not taking any chances."

"I don't think you've got anything to worry about."

"That's reassuring. How awful, though. How god awful for both of them."

"The things people do."

"You said it. Well, what do you want to do? We could sit around feeling sorry for two men and the mess they made of their lives, or we could go back to the hotel and do something life-affirming. You tell me."

"It's a tough one," I said. "How soon do you need my decision?"

LET'S GET LOST

When the phone call came I was parked in front of the television set in the front room, nursing a glass of bourbon and watching the Yankees. It's funny what you remember and what you don't. I remember that Thurman Munson had just hit a long foul that missed being a home run by no more than a foot, but I don't remember who they were playing, or even what kind of a season they had that year.

I remember that the bourbon was J. W. Dant, and that I was drinking it on the rocks, but of course I would remember that. I always remembered what I was drinking, though I didn't always remember why.

The boys had stayed up to watch the opening innings with me, but tomorrow was a school day, and Anita took them upstairs and tucked them in while I freshened my drink and sat down again. The ice was mostly melted by the time Munson hit his long foul, and I was still shaking my head at that when the phone rang. I let it ring, and Anita answered it and came in to tell me it was for me. Somebody's secretary, she said.

I picked up the phone, and a woman's voice, crisply professional, said, "Mr. Scudder, I'm calling for Mr. Alan Herdig of Herdig and Crowell."

"I see," I said, and listened while she elaborated, and estimated just how much time it would take me to get to their offices. I hung up and made a face.

"You have to go in?"

I nodded. "It's about time we had a break in this one," I said. "I don't expect to get much sleep tonight, and I've got a court appearance tomorrow morning."

"I'll get you a clean shirt. Sit down. You've got time to finish your drink, don't you?"

I always had time for that.

Years ago, this was. Nixon was president, a couple of years into his first term. I was a detective with the NYPD, attached to the Sixth Precinct in Greenwich Village. I had a house on Long Island with two cars in the garage, a Ford wagon for Anita and a beat-up Plymouth Valiant for me.

Traffic was light on the LIE, and I didn't pay much attention to the speed limit. I didn't know many cops who did. Nobody ever ticketed a brother officer. I made good time, and it must have been somewhere around a quarter to ten when I left the car at a bus stop on First Avenue. I had a card on the dashboard that would keep me safe from tickets and tow trucks.

The best thing about enforcing the laws is that you don't have to pay a lot of attention to them yourself.

Her doorman rang upstairs to announce me, and she met me at the door with a drink. I don't remember what she was wearing, but I'm sure she looked good in it. She always did.

She said, "I would never call you at home. But it's business."

"Yours or mine?"

"Maybe both. I got a call from a client. A Madison Avenue guy, maybe an agency vice-president. Suits from Tripler's, season tickets for the Rangers, house in Connecticut."

"And?"

"And didn't I say something about knowing a cop? Because he and some friends were having a friendly card game and something happened to one of them."

"Something happened? Something happens to a friend of yours, you take him to a hospital. Or was it too late for that?"

"He didn't say, but that's what I heard. It sounds to me as though somebody had an accident and they need somebody to make it disappear."

"And you thought of me."

"Well," she said.

She'd thought of me before, in a similar connection. Another client of hers, a Wall Street warrior, had had a heart attack in her bed one afternoon. Most men will tell you that's how they want to go, and perhaps it's as good a way as any, but it's not all that convenient for the people who have to clean up after them, especially when the bed in question belongs to some working girl.

When the equivalent happens in the heroin trade, it's good PR. One junkie checks out with an overdose and the first thing all his buddies want to know is where did he get the stuff and how can they cop some themselves. Because, hey, it must be good, right? A hooker, on the other hand, has less to gain from being listed as cause of death. And I suppose she felt a professional responsibility, if you want to call it that, to spare the guy and his family embarrassment. So I made him disappear, and left him

fully dressed in an alley down in the financial district. I
called it in anonymously and went back to her apartment
to claim my reward.

"I've got the address," she said now. "Do you want
to have a look? Or should I tell them I couldn't reach
you?"

I kissed her, and we clung to each other for a long
moment. When I came up for air I said, "It'd be a lie."

"I beg your pardon?"

"Telling them you couldn't reach me. You can always
reach me."

"You're a sweetie."

"You better give me that address," I said.

I retrieved my car from the bus stop and left it in another
one a dozen or so blocks uptown. The address I was
looking for was a brownstone in the East Sixties. A shop
with handbags and briefcases in the window occupied
the storefront, flanked by a travel agent and a men's
clothier. There were four doorbells in the vestibule, and
I rang the third one and heard the intercom activated,
but didn't hear anyone say anything. I was reaching to
ring a second time when the buzzer sounded. I pushed
the door open and walked up three flights of carpeted
stairs.

Out of habit, I stood to the side when I knocked. I
didn't really expect a bullet, and what came through the
door was a voice, pitched low, asking who was there.

"Police," I said. "I understand you've got a situation
here."

There was a pause. Then a voice — maybe the same
one, maybe not — said, "I don't understand. Has there
been a complaint, Officer?"

They wanted a cop, but not just any cop. "My name's

Scudder," I said. "Elaine Mardell said you could use some help."

The lock turned and the door opened. Two men were standing there, dressed for the office in dark suits and white shirts and ties. I looked past them and saw two more men, one in a suit, the other in gray slacks and a blue blazer. They looked to be in their early to mid forties, which made them ten to fifteen years older than me.

I was what, thirty-two that year? Something like that.

"Come on in," one of them said. "Careful."

I didn't know what I was supposed to be careful of, but found out when I gave the door a shove and it stopped after a few inches. There was a body on the floor, a man, curled on his side. One arm was flung up over his head, the other bent at his side, the hand inches from the handle of the knife. It was an easy-open stiletto and it was buried hilt-deep in his chest.

I pushed the door shut and knelt down for a close look at him, and heard the bolt turn as one of them locked the door.

The dead man was around their age, and had been similarly dressed until he took off his suit jacket and loosened his tie. His hair was a little longer than theirs, perhaps because he was losing hair on the crown and wanted to conceal the bald spot. Everyone tries that, and it never works.

I didn't feel for a pulse. A touch of his forehead established that he was too cold to have one. And I hadn't really needed to touch him to know that he was dead. Hell, I knew that much before I parked the car.

Still, I took some time looking him over. Without glancing up I asked what had happened. There was a pause while they decided who would reply, and then the same man who'd questioned me through the closed door said, "We don't really know."

"You came home and found him here?"

"Hardly that. We were playing a few hands of poker, the five of us. Then the doorbell rang and Phil went to see who it was."

I nodded at the dead man. "That's Phil there?"

Someone said it was. "He'd folded already," the man in the blazer added.

"And the rest of you fellows were still in the middle of a hand."

"That's right."

"So he — Phil?"

"Yes, Phil."

"Phil went to the door while you finished the hand."

"Yes."

"And?"

"And we didn't really see what happened," one of the suits said.

"We were in the middle of a hand," another explained, "and you can't really see much from where we were sitting."

"At the card table," I said.

"That's right."

The table was set up at the far end of the living room. It was a poker table, with a green baize top and wells for chips and glasses. I walked over and looked at it.

"Seats eight," I said.

"Yes."

"But there were only the five of you. Or were there other players as well?"

"No, just the five of us."

"The four of you and Phil."

"Yes."

"And Phil was clear across the room answering the door, and one or two of you would have had your backs to it, and all four of you would have been more interested in the way the hand was going than who was at the door." They nodded along, pleased at my ability to grasp all this. "But you must have heard something that made you look up."

"Yes," the blazer said. "Phil cried out."

"What did he say?"

" 'No!' or 'Stop!' or something like that. That got our attention, and we got out of our chairs and looked over there, but I don't think any of us got a look at the guy."

"The guy who . . ."

"Stabbed Phil."

"He must have been out the door before you had a chance to look at him."

"Yes."

"And pulled the door shut after him."

"Or Phil pushed it shut while he was falling."

I said, "Stuck out a hand to break his fall . . . "

"Right."

"And the door swung shut, and he went right on falling."

"Right."

I retraced my steps to the spot where the body lay. It was a nice apartment, I noted, spacious and comfortably furnished. It felt like a bachelor's full-time residence, not a married commuter's pied-à-terre. There were books on the bookshelves, framed prints on the walls, logs in the fireplace. Opposite the fireplace, a two-by-three throw rug looked out of place atop a large Oriental carpet. I had a hunch I knew what it was doing there.

But I walked past it and knelt down next to the corpse. "Stabbed in the heart," I noted. "Death must have been instantaneous, or the next thing to it. I don't suppose he had any last words."

"No."

"He crumpled up and hit the floor and never moved."

"That's right."

I got to my feet. "Must have been a shock."

"A terrible shock."

"How come you didn't call it in?"

"Call it in?"

"Call the police," I said. "Or an ambulance, get him to a hospital."

"A hospital couldn't do him any good," the blazer said. "I mean, you could tell he was dead."

"No pulse, no breathing."

"Right."

"Still, you must have known you're supposed to call the cops when something like this happens."

'Yes, of course."

"But you didn't."

They looked at each other. It might have been interesting to see what they came up with, but I made it easy for them.

"You must have been scared," I said.

"Well, of course."

"Guy goes to answer the door and the next thing you know he's dead on the floor. That's got to be an upsetting experience, especially taking into account that you don't know who killed him or why. Or do you have an idea?"

They didn't.

"I don't suppose this is Phil's apartment."

"No."

Of course not. If it was, they'd have long since gone their separate ways.

"Must be yours," I told the blazer, and enjoyed it when his eyes widened. He allowed that it was, and asked how I knew. I didn't tell him he was the one man in the room without a wedding ring, or that I figured he'd changed from a business suit to slightly more casual clothes on his return home, while the others were still wearing what they'd worn to the office that morning.

I just muttered something about policemen developing certain instincts, and let him think I was a genius.

I asked if any of them had known Phil very well, and wasn't surprised to learn that they hadn't. He was a friend of a friend of a friend, someone said, and did something on Wall Street.

"So he wasn't a regular at the table."

"No."

"This wasn't his first time, was it?"

"His second," somebody said.

"First time was last week?"

"No, two weeks ago. He didn't play last week."

"Two weeks ago. How'd he do?"

Elaborate shrugs. The consensus seemed to be that he might have won a few dollars, but nobody had paid much attention.

"And this evening?"

"I think he was about even. If he was ahead it couldn't have been more than a few dollars."

"What kind of stakes do you play for?"

"It's a friendly game. One-two-five in stud games. In draw it's two dollars before the draw, five after."

"So you can win or lose what, a couple of hundred?"

"That would be a big loss."

"Or a big win," I said.

"Well, yes. Either way."

I knelt down next to the corpse and patted him down. Cards in his wallet identified him as Philip I. Ryman, with an address in Teaneck.

"Lived in Jersey," I said. "And you say he worked on Wall Street?"

"Somewhere downtown."

I picked up his left hand. His watch was Rolex, and I suppose it must have been a real one; this was before the profusion of fakes. He had what looked like a wedding band on the appropriate finger, but I saw that it was in fact a large silver or white-gold ring that had gotten turned around, so that the large part was on the palm side of his hand. It looked like an unfinished signet ring, waiting for an initial to be carved into its gleaming surface.

I straightened up. "Well," I said, "I'd say it's a good thing you called me."

There are a couple of problems," I told them. "A couple of things that could pop up like a red flag for a responding officer or a medical examiner."

"Like . . ."

"Like the knife," I said. "Phil opened the door and the killer stabbed him once and left, was out the door and down the stairs before the body hit the carpet."

"Maybe not that fast," one of them said, "but it was pretty quick. Before we knew what had happened, certainly."

"I appreciate that," I said, "but the thing is it's an unusual MO. The killer didn't take time to make sure his victim was dead, and you can't take that for granted when you stick a knife in someone. And he left the knife in the wound."

"He wouldn't do that?"

"Well, it might be traced to him. All he has to do to avoid that chance is take it away with him. Besides, it's a weapon. Suppose someone comes chasing after him? He might need that knife again."

"Maybe he panicked."

"Maybe he did," I agreed. "There's another thing, and a medical examiner would notice this if a reporting officer didn't. The body's been moved."

Interesting the way their eyes jumped all over the

place. They looked at each other, they looked at me, they looked at Phil on the floor.

"Blood pools in a corpse," I said. "Lividity's the word they use for it. It looks to me as though Phil fell forward and wound up face downward. He probably fell against the door as it was closing, and slid down and wound up on his face. So you couldn't get the door open, and you needed to, so eventually you moved him."

Eyes darted. The host, the one in the blazer, said, "We knew you'd have to come in."

"Right."

"And we couldn't have him lying against the door."

"Of course not," I agreed. "But all of that's going to be hard to explain. You didn't call the cops right away, and you did move the body. They'll have some questions for you."

"Maybe you could give us an idea what questions to expect."

"I might be able to do better than that," I said. "It's irregular, and I probably shouldn't, but I'm going to suggest an action we can take."

"Oh?"

"I'm going to suggest we stage something," I said. "As it stands, Phil was stabbed to death by an unknown person who escaped without anybody getting a look at him. He may never turn up, and if he doesn't, the cops are going to look hard at the four of you."

"Jesus," somebody said.

"It would be a lot easier on everybody," I said, "if Phil's death was an accident."

"An accident?"

"I don't know if Phil has a sheet or not," I said. "He looks vaguely familiar to me, but lots of people do. He's got a gambler's face, even in death, the kind of face you expect to see in an OTB parlor. He may have worked on

Wall Street, it's possible, because cheating at cards isn't necessarily a full-time job."

"Cheating at cards?"

"That would be my guess. His ring's a mirror; turned around, it gives him a peek at what's coming off the bottom of the deck. It's just one way to cheat, and he probably had thirty or forty others. You think of this as a social event, a once-a-week friendly game, a five-dollar limit and, what, three raises maximum? The wins and losses pretty much average out over the course of a year, and nobody ever gets hurt too bad. Is that about right?"

"Yes."

"So you wouldn't expect to attract a mechanic, a card cheat, but he's not looking for the high rollers, he's looking for a game just like yours, where it's all good friends and nobody's got reason to get suspicious, and he can pick up two or three hundred dollars in a couple of hours without running any risks. I'm sure you're all decent poker players, but would you think to look for bottom dealing or a cold deck? Would you know if somebody was dealing seconds, even if you saw it in slow motion?"

"Probably not."

"Phil was probably doing a little cheating," I went on, "and that's probably what he did two weeks ago, and nobody spotted him. But he evidently crossed someone else somewhere along the line. Maybe he pulled the same tricks in a bigger game, or maybe he was just sleeping in the wrong bed, but someone knew he was coming here, turned up after the game was going, and rang the bell. He would have come in and called Phil out, but he didn't have to, because Phil answered the door."

"And the guy had a knife."

"Right," I said. "That's how it was, but it's another way an investigating officer might get confused. How did the guy know Phil was going to come to the door?

Most times the host opens the door, and the rest of the time it's only one chance in five it'll be Phil. Would the guy be ready, knife in hand? And would Phil just open up without making sure who it was?"

I held up a hand. "I know, that's how it happened. But I think it might be worth your while to stage a more plausible scenario, something a lot easier for the cops to come to terms with. Suppose we forget the intruder. Suppose the story we tell is that Phil was cheating at cards and someone called him on it. Maybe some strong words were said and threats were exchanged. Phil went into his pocket and came out with a knife."

"That's . . ."

"You're going to say it's far-fetched," I said, "but he'd probably have some sort of weapon on him, something to intimidate anyone who did catch him cheating. He pulls the knife and you react. Say you turn the table over on him. The whole thing goes crashing to the floor and he winds up sticking his own knife in his chest."

I walked across the room. "We'll have to move the table," I went on. "There's not really room for that sort of struggle where you've got it set up, but suppose it was right in the middle of the room, under the light fixture? Actually that would be a logical place for it." I bent down, picked up the throw rug, tossed it aside. "You'd move the rug if you had the table here." I bent down, poked at a stain. "Looks like somebody had a nosebleed, and fairly recently, or you'd have had the carpet cleaned by now. That can fit right in, come to think of it. Phil wouldn't have bled much from a stab wound to the heart, but there'd have been a little blood loss, and I didn't spot any blood at all where the body's lying now. If we put him in the right spot, they'll most likely assume it's his blood, and it might even turn out to be the same blood type. I mean, there are only so many blood types, right?"

I looked at them one by one. "I think it'll work,"

I said. "To sweeten it, we'll tell them you're friends of mine. I play in this game now and then, although I wasn't here when Phil was. And when the accident happened the first thing you thought of was to call me, and that's why there was a delay reporting the incident. You'd reported it to me, and I was on my way here, and you figured that was enough." I stopped for breath, took a moment to look each of them in the eye. "We'll want things arranged just right," I went on, "and it'll be a good idea to spread a little cash around. But I think this one'll go into the books as accidental death."

"They must have thought you were a genius," Elaine said.

"Or an idiot savant," I said. "Here I was, telling them to fake exactly what had in fact happened. At the beginning I think they may have thought I was blundering into an unwitting reconstruction of the incident, but by the end they probably figured out that I knew where I was going. "

"But you never spelled it out."

"No, we maintained the fiction that some intruder stuck the knife in Ryman, and we were tampering with the evidence."

"When actually you were restoring it. What tipped you off?"

"The body blocking the door. The lividity pattern was wrong, but I was suspicious even before I confirmed that. It's just too cute, a body positioned where it'll keep a door from opening. And the table was in the wrong place, and the little rug had to be covering something, or why else would it be where it was? So I pictured the room the right way, and then everything sort of filled in. But it didn't take a genius. Any cop would have seen some wrong things, and he'd have asked a few hard questions, and the four of them would have caved in."

"And then what? Murder indictments?"

"Most likely, but they're respectable businessmen and the deceased was a scumbag, so they'd have been up on manslaughter charges and probably would have pleaded to a lesser charge. Still, a verdict of accidental death saves them a lot of aggravation. "

"And that's what really happened?"

"I can't see any of those men packing a switch knife, or pulling it at a card table. Nor does it seem likely they could have taken it away from Ryman and killed him with it. I think he went ass over teakettle with the table coming down on top of him and maybe one or two of the guys falling on top of the table. And he was still holding the knife, and he stuck it in his own chest."

"And the cops who responded — "

"Well, I called it in for them, so I more or less selected the responding officers. I picked guys you can work with."

"And worked with them."

"Everybody came out okay," I said. "I collected a few dollars from the four players, and I laid off some of it where it would do the most good."

"Just to smooth things out."

"That's right."

"But you didn't lay off all of it."

"No," I said, "not quite all of it. Give me your hand. Here."

"What's this?"

"A finder's fee."

"Three hundred dollars?"

"Ten percent," I said.

"Gee," she said. "I didn't expect anything."

"What do you do when somebody gives you money?"

"I say thank you," she said, "and I put it someplace safe. This is great. You get them to tell the truth, and everybody gets paid. Do you have to go back to Syosset right away? Because Chet Baker's at Mikell's tonight."

"We could go hear him," I said, "and then we could come back here. I told Anita I'd probably have to stay over."

"Oh, goodie," she said. "Do you suppose he'll sing 'Let's Get Lost'?"

"I wouldn't be surprised," I said. "Not if you ask him nice."

I don't remember if he sang it or not, but I heard it again just the other day on the radio. He'd ended abruptly, that aging boy with the sweet voice and sweeter horn. He went out a hotel room window somewhere in Europe, and most people figured he'd had help. He'd crossed up a lot of people along the way and always got away with it, but then that's usually the way it works. You dodge all the bullets but the last one.

"Let's Get Lost." I heard the song, and not twenty-four hours later I picked up the *Times* and read an obit for a commodities trader named P. Gordon Fawcett, who'd succumbed to prostate cancer. The name rang a bell, but it took me hours to place it. He was the guy in the blazer, the man in whose apartment Phil Ryman stabbed himself.

Funny how things work out. It wasn't too long after that poker game that another incident precipitated my departure from the NYPD, and from my marriage. Elaine and I lost track of each other, and caught up with each other some years down the line, by which time I'd found a way to live without drinking. So we got lost and found — and now we're married. Who'd have guessed?

My life's vastly different these days, but I can imagine being called in on just that sort of emergency — a man dead on the carpet, a knife in his chest, in the company of four poker players who only wish he'd disappear. As I said, my life's different, and I suppose I'm different myself. So I'd almost certainly handle it differently now, and what I'd probably do is call it in immediately and let the cops deal with it.

Still, I always liked the way that one worked out. I walked in on a cover-up, and what I did was cover up the cover-up. And in the process I wound up with the truth. Or an approximation of it, at least, and isn't that as much as you can expect to get? Isn't that enough?

A MOMENT OF WRONG THINKING

Monica said, "What kind of a gun? A man shoots himself in his living room, surrounded by his nearest and dearest, and you want to know what kind of a gun he used?"

"I just wondered," I said.

Monica rolled her eyes. She's one of Elaine's oldest friends. They were in high school together, in Rego Park, and they never lost touch over the years. Elaine spent a lot of years as a call girl, and Monica, who was never in the life herself, seemed to have no difficulty accepting that. Elaine, for her part, had no judgment on Monica's predilection for dating married men.

She was with the current one that evening. The four of us had gone to a revival of *Allegro*, the Rodgers and Hammerstein show that hadn't been a big hit the first time around. From there we went to Paris Green for a late supper. We talked about the show and speculated on reasons for its limited success. The songs were good, we agreed, and I was old enough to remember hearing

"A Fellow Needs a Girl" on the radio. Elaine said she had a Lisa Kirk LP, and one of the cuts was "The Gentleman Is a Dope." That number, she said, had stopped the show during its initial run, and launched Lisa Kirk.

Monica said she'd love to hear it sometime. Elaine said all she had to do was find the record and then find something to play it on. Monica said she still had a turntable for LPs.

Monica's guy didn't say anything, and I had the feeling he didn't know who Lisa Kirk was, or why he had to go through all this just to get laid. His name was Doug Halley — like the comet, he'd said — and he did something in Wall Street. Whatever it was, he did well enough at it to keep his second wife and their kids in a house in Pound Ridge, in Westchester County, while he was putting the kids from his first marriage through college. He had a boy at Bowdoin, we'd learned, and a girl who'd just started at Colgate.

We got as much conversational mileage as we could out of Lisa Kirk, and the drinks came — Perrier for me, cranberry juice for Elaine and Monica, and a Stolichnaya martini for Halley. He'd hesitated for a beat before ordering it — Monica would surely have told him I was a sober alcoholic, and even if she hadn't he'd have noted that he was the only one drinking — and I could almost hear him think it through and decide the hell with it. I was just as glad he'd ordered the drink. He looked as though he needed it, and when it came he drank deep.

It was about then that Monica mentioned the fellow who'd shot himself. It had happened the night before, too late to make the morning papers, and Monica had seen the coverage that afternoon on New York One. A man in Inwood, in the course of a social evening at his own home, with friends and family members present, had drawn a gun, ranted about his financial situation and everything that was wrong with the world, and then stuck the gun in his mouth and blown his brains out.

"What kind of a gun," Monica said again. "It's a guy thing, isn't it? There's not a woman in the world who would ask that question."

"A woman would ask what he was wearing," Halley said.

"No," Elaine said. "Who cares what he was wearing? A woman would ask what his wife was wearing."

"A look of horror would be my guess," Monica said. "Can you imagine? You're having a nice evening with friends and your husband shoots himself in front of everybody?"

"They didn't show it, did they?"

"They didn't interview her on camera, but they did talk with some man who was there and saw the whole thing."

Halley said that it would have been a bigger story if they'd had the wife on camera, and we started talking about the media and how intrusive they'd become. And we stayed with that until they brought us our food.

When we got home Elaine said, "The man who shot himself. When you asked if they showed it, you didn't mean an interview with the wife. You wanted to know if they showed him doing it."

"These days," I said, "somebody's almost always got a camcorder running. But I didn't really think anybody had the act on tape."

"Because it would have been a bigger story."

"That's right. The play a story gets depends on what they've got to show you. It would have been a little bigger than it was if they'd managed to interview the wife, but it would have been everybody's lead story all day long if they could have actually shown him doing it."

"Still, you asked."

"Idly," I said. "Making conversation."

"Yeah, right. And you want to know what kind of gun he used. Just being a guy, and talking guy talk. Because you liked Doug so much, and wanted to bond with him."

"Oh, I was crazy about him. Where does she find them?"

"I don't know," she said, "but I think she's got radar. If there's a jerk out there, and if he's married, she homes in on him. What did you care what kind of gun it was?"

"What I was wondering," I said, "was whether it was a revolver or an automatic."

She thought about it. "And if they showed him doing it, you could look at the film and know what kind of a gun it was."

"Anybody could."

"I couldn't," she said. "Anyway, what difference does it make?"

"Probably none."

"Oh?"

"It reminded me of a case we had," I said. "Ages ago."

"Back when you were a cop, and I was a cop's girlfriend."

I shook my head. "Only the first half. I was on the force, but you and I hadn't met yet. I was still wearing a uniform, and it would be a while before I got my gold shield. And we hadn't moved to Long Island yet, we were still living in Brooklyn."

"You and Anita and the boys."

"Was Andy even born yet? No, he couldn't have been, because she was pregnant with him when we bought the house in Syosset. We probably had Mike by then, but what difference does it make? It wasn't about them. It was about the poor son of a bitch in Park Slope who shot himself."

"And did he use a revolver or an automatic?"

"An automatic. He was a World War Two vet, and this was the gun he'd brought home with him. It must have been a forty-five."

"And he stuck it in his mouth and — "

"Put it to his temple. Putting it in your mouth, I think it was cops who made that popular."

"Popular?"

"You know what I mean. The expression caught on, 'eating your gun,' and you started seeing more civilian suicides who took that route." I fell silent, remembering. "I was partnered with Vince Mahaffey. I've told you about him."

"He smoked those little cigars."

"Guinea-stinkers, he called them. DeNobilis was the brand name, and they were these nasty little things that looked as though they'd passed through the digestive system of a cat. I don't think they could have smelled any worse if they had. Vince smoked them all day long, and he ate like a pig and drank like a fish."

"The perfect role model."

"Vince was all right," I said. "I learned a hell of a lot from Vince."

"Are you gonna tell me the story?"

"You want to hear it?"

She got comfortable on the couch. "Sure," she said. "I like it when you tell me stories."

It was a week night, I remembered, and the moon was full. It seems to me it was in the spring, but I could be wrong about that part.

Mahaffey and I were in a radio car. I was driving when the call came in, and he rang in and said we'd take this one. It was in the Slope. I don't remember the address, but wherever it was we weren't far from it, and I drove there and we went in.

Park Slope's a very desirable area now, but this was before the gentrification process got underway, and the Slope was still a working-class neighborhood, and predominantly Irish. The house we were directed to was one of a row of identical brownstone houses, four stories tall, two apartments to a floor. The vestibule was a half-flight up from street level, and a man was standing in the doorway, waiting for us.

"You want the Conways," he said. "Two flights up and on your left."

"You're a neighbor?"

"Downstairs of them," he said. "It was me called it in. My wife's with her now, the poor woman. He was a bastard, that husband of hers."

"You didn't get along?"

"Why would you say that? He was a good neighbor."

"Then how did he get to be a bastard?"

"To do what he did," the man said darkly. "You want to kill yourself, Jesus, it's an unforgivable sin, but it's a man's own business, isn't it?" He shook his head. "But do it in private, for God's sake. Not with your wife looking on. As long as the poor woman lives, that's her last memory of her husband."

We climbed the stairs. The building was in good repair, but drab, and the stairwell smelled of cabbage and of mice. The cooking smells in tenements have changed over the years, with the ethnic makeup of their occupants. Cabbage was what you used to smell in Irish neighborhoods. I suppose it's still much in evidence in Greenpoint and Brighton Beach, where new arrivals from Poland and Russia reside. And I'm sure the smells are very different in the stairwells of buildings housing immigrants from Asia and Africa and Latin America, but I suspect the mouse smell is there, too.

Halfway up the second flight of stairs, we met a woman on her way down. "Mary Frances!" she called upstairs. "It's the police!" She turned to us. "She's in the back," she said, "with her kids, the poor darlings. It's just at the top of the stairs, on your left. You can walk right in."

The door of the Conway apartment was ajar. Mahaffey knocked on it, then pushed it open when the knock went unanswered. We walked in and there he was, a middle-aged man in dark blue trousers and a white cotton tank-top undershirt. He'd nicked himself shaving that morning, but that was the least of his problems.

He was sprawled in an easy chair facing the television set. He'd fallen over on his left side, and there was a large hole in his right temple, the skin scorched around the entry wound. His right hand lay in his lap, the fingers still holding the gun he'd brought back from the war.

"Jesus," Mahaffey said.

There was a picture of Jesus on the wall over the fireplace, and, similarly framed, another of John F. Kennedy. Other photos and holy pictures reposed here and there in the room — on tabletops, on walls, on top of the television set. I was looking at a small framed photo of a smiling young man in an army uniform and just beginning to realize it was a younger version of the dead man when his wife came into the room.

"I'm sorry," she said, "I never heard you come in. I was with the children. They're in a state, as you can imagine."

"You're Mrs. Conway?"

"Mrs. James Conway." She glanced at her late husband, but her eyes didn't stay on him for long. "He was talking and laughing," she said. "He was making jokes. And then he shot himself. Why would he do such a thing?"

"Had he been drinking, Mrs. Conway?"

"He'd had a drink or two," she said. "He liked his drink. But he wasn't drunk."

"Where'd the bottle go?"

She put her hands together. She was a small woman, with a pinched face and pale blue eyes, and she wore a cotton housedress with a floral pattern. "I put it away," she said. "I shouldn't have done that, should I?"

"Did you move anything else, ma'am?"

"Only the bottle," she said. "The bottle and the glass. I didn't want people saying he was drunk when he did it, because how would that be for the children?" Her face clouded. "Or is it better thinking it was the drink that made him do it? I don't know which is worse. What do you men think?"

"I think we could all use a drink," he said. "Yourself not least of all, ma'am."

She crossed the room and got a bottle of Schenley's from a mahogany cabinet. She brought it, along with three small glasses of cut crystal. Mahaffey poured drinks for all three of us and held his to the light. She took a tentative sip of hers while Mahaffey and I drank ours down. It was an ordinary blended whiskey, an honest workingman's drink. Nothing fancy about it, but it did the job.

Mahaffey raised his glass again and looked at the bare-bulb ceiling fixture through it. "These are fine glasses," he said.

"Waterford," she said. "There were eight, they were

my mother's, and these three are all that's left." She glanced at the dead man. "He had his from a jelly glass. We don't use the Waterford for every day."

"Well, I'd call this a special occasion," Mahaffey said. "Drink that yourself, will you? It's good for you."

She braced herself, drank the whiskey down, shuddered slightly, then drew a deep breath. "Thank you," she said. "It *is* good for me, I'd have to say. No, no more for me. But have another for yourselves."

I passed. Vince poured himself a short one. He went over her story with her, jotting down notes from time to time in his notebook. At one point she began to calculate how she'd manage without poor Jim. He'd been out of work lately, but he was in the building trades, and when he worked he made decent money. And there'd be something from the Veterans Administration, wouldn't there? And Social Security?

"I'm sure there'll be something," Vince told her. "And insurance? Did he have insurance?"

There was a policy, she said. Twenty-five thousand dollars, he'd taken it out when the first child was born, and she'd seen to it that the premium was paid each month. But he'd killed himself, and wouldn't that keep them from paying?

"That's what everybody thinks," he told her, "but it's rarely the case. There's generally a clause, no payment for suicide during the first six months, the first year, maybe even the first two years. To keep you from taking out the policy on Monday and doing away with yourself on Tuesday. But you've had this for more than two years, haven't you?"

She was nodding eagerly. "How old is Patrick? Almost nine, and it was taken out just around the time he was born."

"Then I'd say you're in the clear," he said. "And

it's only fair, if you think about it. The company's been taking a man's premiums all these years, why should a moment of wrong thinking get them off the hook?"

"I had the same notion myself," she said, "but I thought there was no hope. I thought that was just the way it was."

"Well," he said, "it's not."

"What did you call it? A moment of wrong thinking? But isn't that all it takes to keep him out of heaven? It's the sin of despair, you know." She addressed this last to me, guessing that Mahaffey was more aware of the theology of it than I. "And is that fair?" she demanded, turning to Mahaffey again. "Better to cheat a widow out of the money than to cheat James Conway into hell."

"Maybe the Lord's able to take a longer view of things."

"That's not what the fathers say."

"If he wasn't in his right mind at the time . . ."

"His right mind!" She stepped back, pressed her hand to her breast. "Who in his right mind ever did such a thing?"

"Well . . ."

"He was joking," she said. "And he put the gun to his head, and even then I wasn't frightened, because he seemed his usual self and there was nothing frightening about it. Except I had the thought that the gun might go off by accident, and I said as much."

"What did he say to that?"

"That we'd all be better off if it did, himself included. And I said not to say such a thing, that it was horrid and sinful, and he said it was only the truth, and then he looked at me, he *looked* at me."

"What kind of a look?"

"Like, See what I'm doing? Like, Are you watching me, Mary Frances? And then he shot himself."

"Maybe it was an accident," I suggested.

"I saw his face. I saw his finger tighten on the trigger. It was as if he did it to spite me. But he wasn't angry at me. For the love of God, why would he . . ."

Mahaffey clapped me on the shoulder. "Take Mrs. Conway into the other room," he said. "Let her freshen up her face and drink a glass of water, and make sure the kids are all right." I looked at him, and he gave my shoulder a squeeze. "Something I want to check," he said.

I went into the kitchen, where Mrs. Conway wet a dish towel and dabbed tentatively at her face, then filled a jelly glass with water and drank it down in a series of small sips. Then we went to check on the children, a boy of eight and a girl a couple of years younger. They were just sitting there, hands folded in their laps, as if someone had told them not to move.

Mrs. Conway fussed over them and assured them everything was going to be fine and told them to get ready for bed. We left them as we found them, sitting side by side, their hands still folded in their laps. I suppose they were in shock, and it seemed to me they had the right.

I brought the woman back to the living room, where Mahaffey was bent over the body of her husband. He straightened up as we entered the room. "Mrs. Conway," he said, "I have something important to tell you."

She waited to hear what it was.

"Your husband didn't kill himself," he announced.

Her eyes widened, and she looked at Mahaffey as if he'd gone suddenly mad. "But I saw him do it," she said.

He frowned, nodded. "Forgive me," he said. "I misspoke. What I meant to say was that the poor man did not commit suicide. He did kill himself, of course he killed himself — "

"I saw him do it."

" — and of course you did, and what a terrible thing for you, what a cruel thing. But it was not his intention, ma'am. It was an accident."

"An accident!"

"Yes."

"To put a gun to your head and pull the trigger. An accident?"

Mahaffey had a handkerchief in his hand. He turned his hand palm up to show what he was holding with it. It was the cartridge clip from the pistol.

"An accident," Mahaffey said. "You said he was joking, and that's what it was, a joke that went bad. Do you know what this is?"

"Something to do with the gun?"

"It's the clip, ma'am. Or the magazine, they call it that as well. It holds the cartridges."

"The bullets?"

"The bullets, yes. And do you know where I found it?"

"In the gun?"

"That's where I would have expected to find it," he said, "and that's where I looked for it, but it wasn't there. And then I patted his pants pockets, and there it was." And, still using the handkerchief to hold it, he tucked the cartridge clip into the man's right-hand pocket.

"You don't understand," he told the woman. "How about you, Matt? You see what happened?"

"I think so."

"He was playing a joke on you, ma'am. He took the clip out of the gun and put it in his pocket. Then he was going to hold the unloaded gun to his head and give you a scare. He'd give the trigger a squeeze, and there'd be that instant before the hammer clicked on an empty chamber, that instant where you'd think he'd really shot himself, and he'd get to see your reaction."

"But he did shoot himself," she said.

"Because the gun still had a round in the chamber. Once you've chambered a round, removing the clip won't unload the gun. He forgot about the round in the chamber, he thought he had an unloaded weapon in his hand, and when he squeezed the trigger he didn't even have time to be surprised."

"Christ have mercy," she said.

"Amen to that," Mahaffey said. "It's a horrible thing, ma'am, but it's not suicide. Your husband never meant to kill himself. It's a tragedy, a terrible tragedy, but it was an accident." He drew a breath. "It might cost him a bit of time in purgatory, playing a joke like that, but he's spared hellfire, and that's something, isn't it? And now I'll want to use your phone, ma'am, and call this in."

"That's why you wanted to know if it was a revolver or an automatic," Elaine said. "One has a clip and one doesn't."

"An automatic has a clip. A revolver has a cylinder."

"If he'd had a revolver he could have played Russian roulette. That's when you spin the cylinder, isn't it?"

"So I understand."

"How does it work? All but one chamber is empty? Or all but one chamber has a bullet in it?"

"I guess it depends what kind of odds you like."

She thought about it, shrugged. "These poor people in Brooklyn," she said. "What made Mahaffey think of looking for the clip?"

"Something felt off about the whole thing," I said, "and he remembered a case of a man who'd shot a friend with what he was sure was an unloaded gun, because he'd removed the clip. That was the defense at trial, he told me, and it hadn't gotten the guy anywhere, but it stayed in Mahaffey's mind. And as soon as he took a close look at the gun he saw the clip was missing, so it was just a matter of finding it."

"In the dead man's pocket."

"Right."

"Thus saving James Conway from an eternity in hell," she said. "Except he'd be off the hook with or without Mahaffey, wouldn't he? I mean, wouldn't God know where to send him without having some cop hold up a cartridge clip?"

"Don't ask me, honey. I'm not even Catholic."

"Goyim is goyim," she said. "You're supposed to know these things. Never mind, I get the point. It may not make a difference to God or to Conway, but it makes a real difference to Mary Frances. She can bury her husband in holy ground and know he'll be waiting for her when she gets to heaven her own self."

"Right."

"It's a terrible story, isn't it? I mean, it's a good story as a story, but it's terrible, the idea of a man killing himself that way. And his wife and kids witnessing it, and having to live with it."

"Terrible," I agreed.

"But there's more to it. Isn't there?"

"More?"

"Come on," she said. "You left something out."

"You know me too well."

"Damn right I do."

"So what's the part I didn't get to?"

She thought about it. "Drinking a glass of water," she said.

"How's that?"

"He sent you both out of the room," she said, "*before* he looked to see if the clip was there or not. So it was just Mahaffey, finding the clip all by himself."

"She was beside herself, and he figured it would do

her good to splash a little water on her face. And we hadn't heard a peep out of those kids, and it made sense to have her check on them."

"And she had to have you along so she didn't get lost on the way to the bedroom. "

I nodded. "It's convenient," I allowed, "making the discovery with no one around. He had plenty of time to pick up the gun, remove the clip, put the gun back in Conway's hand, and slip the clip into the man's pocket. That way he could do his good deed for the day, turning a suicide into an accidental death. It might not fool God, but it would be more than enough to fool the parish priest. Conway's body could be buried in holy ground, regardless of his soul's ultimate destination."

"And you think that's what he did?"

"It's certainly possible. But suppose you're Mahaffey, and you check the gun and the clip's still in it, and you do what we just said. Would you stand there with the clip in your hand waiting to tell the widow and your partner what you learned?"

"Why not?" she said, and then answered her own question. "No, of course not," she said. "If I'm going to make a discovery like that I'm going to do so in the presence of witnesses. What I do, I get the clip, I take it out, I slip it in his pocket, I put the gun back in his hand, and *then* I wait for the two of you to come back. And then I get a bright idea, and we examine the gun and find the clip missing, and one of us finds it in his pocket, where I know it is because that's where I stashed it a minute ago."

"A lot more convincing than his word on what he found when no one was around to see him find it."

"On the other hand," she said, "wouldn't he do that either way? Say I look at the gun and see the clip's missing. Why don't I wait until you come back before I even look for the clip?"

"Your curiosity's too great."

"So I can't wait a minute? But even so, suppose I look and I find the clip in his pocket. Why take it out?"

"To make sure it's what you think it is."

"And why not put it back?"

"Maybe it never occurs to you that anybody would doubt your word," I suggested. "Or maybe, wherever Mahaffey found the clip, in the gun or in Conway's pocket where he said he found it, maybe he would have put it back if he'd had enough time. But we came back in, and there he was with the clip in his hand."

"In his handkerchief, you said. On account of fingerprints?"

"Sure. You don't want to disturb existing prints or leave prints of your own. Not that the lab would have spent any time on this one. They might nowadays, but back in the early sixties? A man shoots himself in front of witnesses?"

She was silent for a long moment. Then she said, "So what happened?"

"What happened?"

"Yeah, your best guess. What really happened?"

"No reason it couldn't have been just the way he reconstructed it. Accidental death. A dumb accident, but an accident all the same."

"But?"

"But Vince had a soft heart," I said. "Houseful of holy pictures like that, he's got to figure it's important to the woman that her husband's got a shot at heaven. If he could fix that up, he wouldn't care a lot about the objective reality of it all."

"And he wouldn't mind tampering with evidence?"

"He wouldn't lose sleep over it. God knows I never did."

"Anybody you ever framed," she said, "was guilty."

"Of something," I agreed. "You want my best guess, it's that there's no way of telling. As soon as the gimmick occurred to Vince, that the clip might be missing, the whole scenario was set. Either Conway had removed the clip and we were going to find it, or he hadn't and we were going to remove it for him, and *then* find it."

" 'The Lady or the Tiger.' Except not really, because either way it comes out the same. It goes in the books as an accident, whether that's what it was or not."

"That's the idea."

"So it doesn't make any difference one way or the other."

"I suppose not," I said, "but I always hoped it was the way Mahaffey said it was."

"Because you wouldn't want to think ill of him? No, that's not it. You already said he was capable of tampering with evidence, and you wouldn't think ill of him for it, anyway. I give up. Why? Because you don't want Mr. Conway to be in hell?"

"I never met the man," I said, "and it would be presumptuous of me to care where he winds up. But I'd prefer it if the clip was in his pocket where Mahaffey said it was, because of what it would prove."

"That he hadn't meant to kill himself? I thought we just said . . ."

I shook my head. "That she didn't do it."

"Who? The wife?"

"Uh-huh."

"That she didn't do what? Kill him? You think *she* killed him?"

"It's possible."

"But he shot himself," she said. "In front of witnesses. Or did I miss something?"

"That's almost certainly what happened," I said, "but she was one of the witnesses, and the kids were the other witnesses, and who knows what they saw, or if they saw anything at all? Say he's on the couch, and they're all watching TV, and she takes his old war souvenir and puts one in his head, and she starts screaming. 'Ohmigod, look what your father has done! Oh, Jesus Mary and Joseph, Daddy has killed himself!' They were looking at the set, they didn't see dick, but they'll think they did by the time she stops carrying on."

"And they never said what they did or didn't see."

"They never said a word, because we didn't ask them anything. Look, I don't think she did it. The possibility didn't even occur to me until sometime later, and by then we'd closed the case, so what was the point? I never even mentioned the idea to Vince."

"And if you had?"

"He'd have said she wasn't the type for it, and he'd have been right. But you never know. If she didn't do it, he gave her peace of mind. If she did do it, she must have wondered how the cartridge clip migrated from the gun butt to her husband's pocket."

"She'd have realized Mahaffey put it there."

"Uh-huh. And she'd have had twenty-five thousand reasons to thank him for it."

"Huh?"

"The insurance," I said.

"But you said they'd have to pay anyway."

"Double indemnity," I said. "They'd have had to pay the face amount of the policy, but if it's an accident they'd have had to pay double. That's if there was a double-indemnity clause in the policy, and I have no way of knowing whether or not there was. But most policies sold around then, especially relatively small policies, had the clause. The companies liked to write them that way, and the policy holders usually went for them. A fraction more in premiums and twice the payoff? Why not go for it?"

We kicked it around a little. Then she asked about the current case, the one that had started the whole thing. I'd wondered about the gun, I explained, purely out of curiosity. If it was in fact an automatic, and if the clip was in fact in his pocket and not in the gun where you'd expect to find it, surely some cop would have determined as much by now, and it would all come out in the wash.

"That's some story," she said. "And it happened when, thirty-five years ago? And you never mentioned it before?"

"I never thought of it," I said, "not as a story worth telling. Because it's unresolved. There's no way to know what really happened."

"That's all right," she said. "It's still a good story."

The guy in Inwood, it turned out, had used a .38-caliber revolver, and he'd cleaned it and loaded it earlier that same day. No chance it was an accident.

And if I'd never told the story over the years, that's not to say it hadn't come occasionally to mind. Vince Mahaffey and I never really talked about the incident, and I've sometimes wished we had. It would have been nice to know what really happened.

Assuming that's possible, and I'm not sure it is. He had, after all, sent me out of the room before doing whatever it was he did. That suggested he hadn't wanted me to know, so why should I think he'd be quick to tell me after the fact?

No way of knowing. And, as the years pass, I find I like it better that way. I couldn't tell you why, but I do.

MICK BALLOU LOOKS
AT THE BLANK SCREEN

"At first," Mick Ballou said, "I thought the same as everyone else in the country. I thought the fucking cable went out."

We were at Grogan's, the Hell's Kitchen saloon he owns and frequents, and he was talking about the final episode of *The Sopranos,* which ended abruptly with the screen going blank and staying that way for ten or fifteen seconds.

"And then I thought, well, they couldn't think of an ending. But Kristin recalled the time Tony and Bobby were talking of death, and what it would be like, and that you wouldn't even know it when it happened to you. So that was the ending, then. Tony dies, and doesn't even know it."

It was late on a weekday night, and the close-mouthed bartender had already shooed the last of the customers out of the place and put the chairs up on the tables, where they'd be out of the way when someone else mopped the floor in the morning. I'd been out late myself, speaking at an AA meeting in Marine Park, then stopping for coffee on the way home. Elaine met me with a message: Mick had called, and could I meet him around two?

There was a time when most of our evenings started around that time, with him drinking twelve-year-old Jameson while I kept him company with coffee or Coke or water. We'd go until dawn, and then he'd drag me down to St. Bernard's on West 14th Street for the butchers' mass. Nowadays our evenings started and ended earlier, and there weren't enough butchers in the gentrified Meat Market district to fill out a mass, and anyway St. Bernard's itself had given up the ghost, and was now Our Lady of Guadalupe.

And we were older, Mick and I. We got tired and went home to bed.

And now he'd summoned me to discuss the ending of a television series.

He said, "What do you think happens?"

"You're not talking about tv."

He shook his head. "Life. Or the end of it. Is that what it is? A blank screen?"

I talked about near death experiences, all of them remarkably similar, with the consciousness hovering in midair and being invited to go to the light, then making the decision to return to the body. "But there's not a lot of eyewitness testimony," I said, "from the ones who go to the light."

He thought about it, nodded.

"You're a Catholic," I said. "Doesn't the Church tell you what happens?"

"There's things I take their word for," he said, "and things I don't. Kristin thinks you meet your loved ones on the other side. But of course she'd want to think that."

Kristin Hollander had lost her parents in a brutal home invasion, and had met Mick in its aftermath, when I sent him to her house to keep her safe. They'd grown friendly since.

"She has this set that puts you in mind of a movie screen," he said. "We watched the show together and sat around for hours talking about it." He drank whiskey. "There are some I'd not mind seeing again. My brother Dennis, for one. But after a few words about old times, what would we talk about for the rest of eternity?"

I wondered where this was going. He'd called me out in the middle of the night, and I had a feeling he wanted to tell me something, and I was afraid to ask what it was.

And so we drifted into a shared silence, not uncommon during our late evenings together. I was searching for a way to break it, but it was Mick who spoke first.

"There's a favor I have to ask you," he said.

I dreaded hearing it," I told Elaine. "I just knew he was going to tell me he was dying."

"But he's not."

"He wants me to stand up for him. He's getting married. To Kristin."

"I figured that's why he wanted to meet you. So he could tell you. You didn't see it coming?"

"I thought they were just friends."

She gave me a look.

"He's forty years older than she is," I said, "and spent those years tearing up the West Side. No, I didn't see it coming."

"You never noticed the way she looks at him? Or the way he looks at her?"

"I knew they enjoyed each other's company," I said, "but—"

"Oy," she said. "Some detective."

ONE LAST NIGHT AT GROGAN'S

We had dinner at Paris Green, a few blocks south of our apartment on Ninth Avenue. I ordered the sweetbreads, and wondered not for the first time why they were called that, being neither sweet nor bread. Elaine pointed out that Google could clear that up for us in no more than thirty seconds. More like two hours, I told her, by the time I'd run out of other fascinating things to click on.

The fish of the day was Alaskan halibut, and that's what she chose. After many years as a vegetarian, she'd been persuaded by a nutritionist to regard fish as a vegetable. At first she worried it would be the culinary equivalent of a gateway drug, and in no time at all she'd be cracking beef bones and sucking out the marrow. So far she hadn't progressed past fish a couple of times a week.

It was around eight when Gary showed us to our table, and maybe an hour later when we said no to dessert and yes to espresso. It's rare for her to have coffee, especially late in the day, and my surprise must have shown in my face. "It could be a long night," she said. "I figure I'd better be awake for it."

"I can see how much you're looking forward to it."

"About as much as you are. It's got to be like a wake without a corpse. Except last night would have been the wake, so what's this? The burial?"

"I guess."

"I always thought the Irish wake made a lot of sense. Pour down the booze until you can think of something good to say about the deceased. My people cover the mirrors, sit around on hard wooden benches, and stuff themselves with food. I wonder what it was like last night."

"I'm sure he'll tell us."

We finished our coffee, and I signaled our waitress for the check. Gary brought it himself. How many years had we known him? How many years had we been coming here a couple of times a month?

It seemed to me that neither he nor the restaurant had changed. He always looked as though something reminded him of a joke, and the light in his blue eyes hadn't dimmed any. But his beard, still hanging from his long jaw like an oriole's nest, showed some gray now, and his age showed at the corners of his eyes. And it was a night to notice such things.

"I didn't see you last night," he said. "Of course I didn't go over until we closed up shop here. You'd probably headed for home by then."

"That would be—"

"The big fella's place. You're friends, aren't you? Or have I got it wrong, as I so often do?"

"We're close friends," I said. "I didn't realize you knew him that well."

"I don't, not really. But he's part of the neighborhood,

isn't he? I doubt I've been in Grogan's a dozen times in as many years, but I made sure I got there last night."

"Paying your respects," Elaine suggested.

"And watching my neighbors take advantage of the open bar. A sight guaranteed to raise or lower your opinion of the human race, depending where it was to begin with. And, you know, being present for the end of an era, and isn't that the most overused phrase at our command? Every time a sitcom's canceled, someone proclaims it the end of an era."

"And once in a while it is," she said.

"You're thinking of *Seinfeld.*"

"Well, yeah."

"An exception," he said, "that proves the rule. As is the shuttering of Grogan's Open House. A fixture in the local landscape, and soon enough the building will be gone and no one will remember what used to be there. Our town, forever reinventing itself. I heard they made the owner such a good offer that he was willing to risk Mr. B's wrath for selling the building out from under him. And I also heard that Mick owned the building, no matter whose name might be on the deed."

"You hear lots of things," I said.

"You do," he agreed. "I'm pleased to report that the era of hearing things is still going strong."

For longer than I've known him, my friend Mick Ballou has been the proprietor of Grogan's Open House, a Hell's Kitchen saloon at the southeast corner of Tenth Avenue and Fiftieth Street. The place began as a hangout for the neighborhood hoodlums, or at least that segment thereof who pledged some sort of undefined allegiance to the man himself. In recent years it has attained a certain degree of raffish respectability, even as the neighborhood has gentrified around it. The new people who've moved into refurbished tenements or new high–rise condos like to stop in for a draft Guinness and point out what may or may not be bullet holes in the walls.

Mick has always tended to hire Irish lads as bartenders, most of them fresh transplants from Belfast or Derry or Strabane, but a Northern Ireland accent never kept a new man from learning how to make a Wild Mustang or a Novarian Sunset. The new crowd liked bellying up to the bar next to old neighborhood regulars, and a man who'd worked half a century as a subway motorman would be transformed in the telling into a desperate character with blood on his hands. The old fellows didn't mind; they were just trying to make a glass of beer last until the next pension check arrived.

"Don't come on the Friday," Mick had told me. "'Twill be our last night, with the whole of the West Side sure to come out for it. An open bar until the taps run dry, and there'll even be a bit of food."

"And everybody's welcome but me?"

"You would be welcome enough," he said, "but you would hate it, as I expect to hate it myself. I won't have Kristin there, and wouldn't be there my own self had I any choice in the matter. Come on the Saturday, and bring herself."

"Friday's your last night," I said.

"It is. And the following night there'll be none but the four of us. And haven't our best nights always been after closing time?"

We walked down Ninth and over Fiftieth, where the last of the Street Fair vendors were dismantling their booths. "Like nomads in Central Asia," Elaine said. "Packing their yurts and heading for richer grazing."

"A few years back their flocks would have gone hungry here," I said, "or been prey for the local wolves. Now they sell T-shirts and Gap knockoffs and Vietnamese sandwiches, and the block association spends the fees installing security cameras and planting more ginkgo trees."

"And look at the ornamental light posts," she said. "Like the ones we saw in Paris."

Grogan's came into view as we neared Tenth Avenue. The tavern occupied the ground floor, with three levels of rental units above it. All the apartment windows facing the street had big white X's on them, indicating that the building was scheduled for demolition. No light showed behind the X's, and Grogan's looked to be dark as well. I wondered if perhaps Mick had changed his mind and gone home, and then I saw one light glowing dimly through the front door's little window.

We hesitated at the curb, although there were no cars coming, and Elaine responded to my unvoiced thought. "We have to," she said.

Kristin unlocked the door for us. A light glowed softly in a leaded glass shade hanging over a table way in the back. There were four chairs grouped around the table, the only chairs in the room that hadn't been put up on top of other tables. Mick wasn't at the table, and I didn't see him anywhere else, either.

"I'm glad you're here," she said. "So's himself." She rolled her eyes. "'So's himself.' Listen to me, will you? He's in the office, he'll be out in a minute. And now that you're here—"

She arranged a cardboard CLOSED sign so that it covered the window. "Double duty," she said. "Tells them we're closed and keeps them from seeing there's a light on."

"All the world sees you as a Jewish–American Princess," said the former Elaine Mardell. "Yet it's clear you were born to be an Irish saloonkeeper."

"A wee village pub in Donegal," Kristin said. "On the wind–swept shores of Lough Swilly. That's our favorite fantasy. The funny thing is I think I could actually enjoy it well enough. And so could he, for three weeks tops. Then he'd want to put a match to the adorable thatched roof and come home."

She led us to the table. Her drink was iced tea, and we said that sounded good to us, too. Mick's bottle of twelve–year–old Jameson was on the table, along with a glass and a little water pitcher. The Jameson bottle is clear glass, so I could note the color of its contents. I still like the color of good whiskey. Or of bad whiskey, for that matter, because the color doesn't say anything about the quality. All it tells you is that you've got a thirst for it.

Before Kristin was back with our iced tea, Mick had emerged from the office in back, a paper bag in hand. "I had the devil's own time finding a bag to put this in," he said, "as if it would have been a hardship to tuck it under your arm and carry it unwrapped through the streets. We've no place for it in the house, and himself made the mistake of admiring it."

I knew what it was before Elaine got it out of the bag, a 9x12 framed Irish landscape.

"It's Conor Pass in the Dingle peninsula," Kristin said. "It really looks like that, too. I think it's the most beautiful place I've ever been."

"It's a hand–colored steel engraving," Elaine said. "There was no color printing at the time, so there were people who added color one at a time by hand. There's a lost art for you, but then so's steel engraving."

"The few arts not yet lost," Mick said, "have their heads on the chopping block, waiting for technology to lop them off." His hand moved first to the bottle, then to the water pitcher, then back to the bottle; he picked it up and poured a small measure of good Cork whiskey into his glass.

"Quite the affair last night," he said.

"I was going to ask."

"Oh, it was a right hooley. They paid their twenty dollars at the door and for that they got to drink until the well ran dry. 'Twas for the help, you know. I had four men working, and they got to divide just over eight thousand dollars."

"Not bad for a night's work."

"Well, it was a long night, and that crowd kept them hopping. But they had their tips on top of that, and the tips are decent when the drinks are free." He'd had his glass in his hand, and now he took the smallest sip from it. "I stood at the door taking the money, and being asked the same fucking questions all night long. 'Wasn't it terrible that the greedy landlord sold the building out from under me?'"

Kristin laid a hand on his arm. "When all along," she said, "the man himself was the greedy landlord."

"I was the best landlord that ever lived," he said. "Three floors above me packed full with rent–controlled tenants, and the heat bill for the building was higher than its rent roll, and I never even bothered putting in for what rent increases the law allowed me."

"A saint," Elaine said.

"I was that. If the Creator were half the landlord I was, Adam and Eve would never have left Eden. My lot would be late with the rent, they might not pay for months on end, and I gave them no trouble. If there's one thing that'll save me a bit of time in Purgatory, it's how I treated my tenants. And then, as a final sweetener, I gave each of them fifty thousand dollars to move."

I said that was generous.

"I could well afford it. Don't ask what Rosenstein got them to pay for the building."

"I won't."

"I'll tell you anyway. Twenty–one million dollars."

"A nice round sum."

"The sum," he said, "was to be twenty million, which is rounder if not so nice, and then Rosenstein went back to them and said his client was fond of the old English system, and preferred guineas to pounds. Are you familiar with guineas?"

"You don't mean Italians."

"A guinea was a gold coin," he said, "back when they had such an article, and it was the nearest thing to a pound sterling, but with twenty–one shillings instead of twenty. So a price in guineas is five percent higher than the same in pounds. I suspect the notion died out when decimal currency came in, but there was a time when your carriage trade liked prices in guineas. Rosenstein told me he didn't really expect this to work, but that it wouldn't be outrageous enough to kill the deal altogether, and we could always back off and take the twenty. But they paid us in guineas after all."

"And that small lagniappe paid off your tenants."

"It did." He put his glass down. "You'd have thought they'd won the Powerball, and in a sense they had. Of course there was one wee fucker, fourth floor rear on the left, who thought there might be a toy or two left in Santa's sack. 'Oh, I don't know, Mr. Ballou, and where am I gonna move to, and how'll I find something decent that I can afford, and all the expenses of relocation.'"

I could see the shadow of a smile on Kristin's face.

"I looked at him," Mick said, "and did I settle a hand on his shoulder? No, I don't believe I did. I just held him with my eyes, and I lowered my voice, and I said I knew he'd be able to move, and move quickly, as it would be unsafe for him and his loved ones to be in the presence of men whose job it was to knock things down and blow them up. And in the end his was the first apartment vacated. Can you imagine?"

Kristin clasped her hands, looking like Lois Lane. "My hero," she said.

It's not impossible to take me by surprise, but I can't think of anything that did so more utterly than Mick's announcement of his upcoming marriage to Kristin. It was at Grogan's that I learned of it, after some preliminary speculation on what happens after you die. I'd been bracing myself for bad news when he asked me to be his best man.

Elaine swears she saw it coming, and can't imagine how I didn't.

Kristin came into our lives when her parents left theirs, the victims of a particularly horrible home invasion. The madman who orchestrated it wasn't finished; he wanted her and the house and the money, and it didn't stop him when I spiked his first try. He came back a few years later, and didn't miss by much.

I got Mick to babysit her, confident that no one would get past him. They sat in the kitchen of her brownstone. They drank coffee and played cribbage. I suppose they talked, though I couldn't guess what they talked about.

That's the same house in which she discovered her parents' bodies. She went on living there, because she is far tougher at the core than you'd think, and she lives there now as my friend's wife, and if they're as unlikely a couple as Beauty and the Beast, you lose sight of the disparity after a few minutes in their company. He's a big man, hard and forbidding as an Easter Island monolith, and she looks to be a frail and slender slip of a girl. He's forty years her senior. She's a child of privilege, while he's a Hell's Kitchen hoodlum who's killed grown men with his hands.

And she settles her hand on his arm, and beams while he tells his stories.

There was a silence, with an unasked question hovering. Elaine broke the one and asked the other. Did he regret the sale?

"No," he said, and shook his head. "Why should I? I could run it a thousand years and not take twenty million dollars out of it. And if it's a neighborhood institution, and enough people felt they had to say so last night, well, it's one the neighborhood's well off without."

"There's history here," I said.

"There is, and most of it misfortunate. Crimes planned, oaths sworn and broken. You were here on the worst night of all."

"I was remembering it just now."

"How could you not? Two men in the doorway, spraying bullets as if they were watering the flowers. One tosses a bomb, and I can see the arc of it now, and the flash before the sound of it, like lightning before thunder."

The room went still again, until Mick got to his feet. "We need music," he announced. "They were supposed to come this afternoon for the Wurlitzer, the truck from St. Vincent de Paul. The creature's not old enough to be valuable or new enough to be truly useful, but they said they'd find a home for it. If they get here tomorrow or Monday they're welcome to it, assuming I'm here to let them in. On Tuesday the building changes hands, and what's in it belongs to the new owner, and most likely goes into a landfill along with the bricks and floorboards. You haven't any use for it, have you? Or a two–ton Mosler safe? I didn't think so. What would you like to hear?"

Elaine and I shrugged. Kristin said, "Something sad."

"Something sad, is it?"

"Something mournful and Irish."

"Ah," he said. "Sure, that's easily arranged."

I remembered an evening some years earlier. Elaine and I on our way out of the Met at Lincoln Center, the last strains of *La Boheme* still resounding. Elaine in a mood, restless. "She always fucking dies. I don't want to go home. Can we hear more music? Something sad, it's fine if it's sad. It can break my fucking heart if it wants. Just so nobody dies."

We hit a couple of clubs, wound up downtown at Small's, and by the time we got out of there the sun was up. And her mood had lifted.

Irish songs on the ground floor of a Hell's Kitchen tenement may be a far cry from jazz in a Village basement, but it served the same purpose, drawing us down into the mood as a means of easing us through it. I don't remember exactly what Mick selected, but there were Clancy Boys and Dubliners cuts, and some ballads of the 1798 Rising, including a rendition of *Boolavogue* with a clear tenor voice backed by a piper's keening.

That was the last record to play, and it would have

been a hard one to follow. I was put in mind of the Chesterton poem, and trying to remember just how it went when Elaine read my mind and quoted it:

For the great Gaels of Ireland
Are the men that God made mad,
For all their wars are merry,
And all their songs are sad.

"I wonder," Mick said. "Is it just the Irish? Or are we all of us like that, deep in our hearts?" He got to his feet, picked up his bottle and glass. "That's enough whiskey. Is it iced tea you're all drinking? I'll fetch us another pitcher." And to Kristin: "No, don't get up. 'Tis my establishment still. I'll provide the service."

He said, "Will I miss it? The short answer is it's a bar like any other, and I've lost my taste for them, even my own."

"And the long answer?"

He gave it some thought. "I expect I will," he said. "The years pile up, you know. The sheer weight of them has an effect. I wasn't always on the premises, but the place was always here for me." He filled his glass with iced tea, sipped it as if it were whiskey. "The room is full of ghosts tonight. Can you feel it?"

We all nodded.

"And not just the shades of those who died that one bad night. Others as well, whose deaths were somewhere else altogether. Just now I looked over at the bar and saw a little old man in a cloth cap, perched on a stool and nursing a beer. I pointed him out to you once, but you wouldn't remember."

But I did. "Ex–IRA," I said. "If it's the fellow I'm thinking of."

"It is. One of Tom Barry's lads in West Cork he was, and that lot shed enough blood to redden Bantry Bay. When his regular local closed he brought his custom here, and drank a beer or two seven nights a week. And then one night he wasn't here, and then the word came that he was gone. No man lives forever, not even a wee cutthroat from Kenmare."

He pronounced it Ken–mahr. There's a Kenmare Street a few blocks long in NoLita, which is the tag realtors have fastened on a few square blocks north of Little Italy. A Tammany hack called Big Tim Sullivan managed to name it for his mother's home town in County Kerry, but he couldn't make people pronounce it in the Irish fashion. Ken–mair's what they say, if indeed they say the name at all; the residents nowadays are mostly Chinese.

"Andy Buckley," he said. "You remember Andy."

That didn't require an answer. I could hardly have forgotten Andy Buckley.

"He was here on that bad night. Got us into the car and away, the two of us."

"I remember."

"As good behind the wheel of a car as any man I've ever known. And as good with darts. He'd scarcely seem to be paying attention, and with a flick of his wrist he'd put the little feathered creature just where he wanted it."

"He made it look effortless."

"He did. You know, when I had them put this place back together again, I bought a new dartboard and had it installed in the usual place on the back wall. And I found I didn't like seeing it there, and I took it down." He took a deep breath, held it, let it out. "I had no choice," he said.

Andy Buckley had betrayed Mick, his employer and friend. Sold him out, set him up. And I'd been there on a lonely road upstate when Mick took Andy's head in his own big hands and broke his neck.

You remember Andy, he'd said.

"No fucking choice," he said, "and yet it never sat easy with me. Or why would I have had them replace the dartboard? And why would I have taken it down?"

"If they hadn't come round with their offer," he said, "I'd never have closed Grogan's. It never would have occurred to me. But the time's right, you know."

Kristin nodded, and I sensed they'd discussed this point before. Elaine asked what was so right about the timing.

"My life's changed," he said. "In many ways, beyond the miracle that an angel came down from heaven to be my bride."

"How he does go on," Kristin said.

"My business interests," he said, "are all legitimate. The few wide boys I had working for me have moved on, and if they're still doing criminal deeds they're doing them at someone else's behest. I'm a silent partner in several enterprises, and I may have come by my interest by canceling a debt or doing someone an illegal favor, but the businesses themselves are lawful and so is my participation."

"And Grogan's is an anomaly?" Elaine frowned. "I don't see how, exactly. It's evolved like the rest of your life, and it's more a yuppie watering hole than a hangout for hoodlums."

He shook his head. "No, that's not the point. In the bar business there's no end of men looking to cheat you.

Suppliers billing you for undelivered goods, bartenders making themselves your silent partners, hard men practicing extortion and calling it advertising or charity. But I always had a pass, you know, because they knew to be afraid of me. Who'd try to get over on a man with my reputation? Who'd dare to steal from me, or cheat me, or put pressure on me?"

"Whoever did would be taking his life in his hands."

"Once," he said. "Once that was true. Now the lion's old and toothless and wants only to lie by the fire. And sooner or later some lad would make his move, and I'd have to do something about it, something I'd not care to do, something I'm past doing. No, I'm well out of the game." He sighed. "Will I miss it? There's parts of the old life I miss, and it's no shame to admit it. I wouldn't care to have it back, but there's times when I miss it." His eyes found mine. "And you? Is it not the same for you?"

"I wouldn't want it back."

"Not for anything. But do you miss it? The drink, and all that went with it?"

"Yes," I said. "There are times I do."

It was late when we left. Mick turned off the one light, locked up, proclaiming the latter a waste of time. "If anyone wants to come in and take something, what does it matter? None of it's mine anymore."

He had his car, the big silver Cadillac, and dropped us off. Nobody had much to say beyond a few pleasantries as we got out of the car, and the silence held while Elaine and I crossed the Parc Vendome's lobby and ascended in the elevator. She had her key out and let us in, and we checked Voice Mail and email, and she found a coffee cup I'd left beside the computer and returned it to the kitchen.

We tried the Conor Pass engraving in a few spots— in a hallway, in the front room—and decided to defer the decision of where to hang it. Elaine felt it wanted to be seen at close range, so we left it for now, propped against the base of a lamp on the drum–top table.

The little tasks one does, all of them performed in a companionable silence.

And then she said "It wasn't so bad."

"No. It was a good evening, actually."

"I love the two of them so much. Individually and together."

"I know."

"And he's much better off without the place. He'll be fine, don't you think?"

"I think so."

"But it really is, isn't it? The end of an era."

"Like *Seinfeld*?"

She shook her head. "Not quite," she said. "There won't be any reruns."

ABOUT THESE STORIES

I began writing about Matthew Scudder in the early 1970s. My first marriage was in dissolution, and I was living alone in an apartment a block from Columbus Circle. I wrote out a series proposal, my agent made a deal with Dell, and the three books flowed from my typewriter one after another: *The Sins of the Fathers, Time to Murder and Create,* and *In the Midst of Death.*

Paperback distribution in general was problematic during those years, and Dell's troubles were greater than most; they returned much of their manuscript inventory, paid for but unpublished, to authors and agents, and but for the personal enthusiasm of editor Bill Grose, Scudder might never have seen print.

The books were published, but distribution was spotty and sales slow, though people who read them seemed to like them well enough. Paperback originals don't often get reviewed, but the three Scudder novels did receive a fair amount of critical attention, and *Time to Murder and Create* was shortlisted for an Edgar Allan Poe award.

But there was certainly no enthusiasm for continuing the series beyond the initial three books, and no reason to believe another publisher would want to take it over. It certainly looked as though I'd be well advised to turn my attention to other books, with other characters.

Scudder, I found, was not that easily abandoned. And so in 1977 I started writing a short story about him, "Out the Window," and it ran long enough for us to call it a novelette. *Alfred Hitchcock's Mystery Magazine* ran it in their September issue, and two months later they printed another, "A Candle for the Bag Lady." (The latter was briefly retitled "Like a Lamb to Slaughter," so that it might serve as the flagship story of a collection with that title, and that's a story in itself—but one I'll save for another time.)

Those two novelettes helped keep the character alive for me. A couple of years later I took a chance and wrote a fourth full-length Scudder novel on spec, and Don Fine published it at Arbor House. That was *A Stab in the Dark,* followed in fairly short order by *Eight Million Ways to Die.*

That was a pivotal volume, for me and for Matthew Scudder. It was twice as long as the early books, and was as much about the dynamics of alcoholism and the general frailty of human existence as it was about the particular murder investigation which drove the plot. The book got a lot of critical attention; it was shortlisted for an Edgar and won a Shamus award outright. But while it looked like the start of something big, the party appeared to be over.

Because how could I go on writing about Scudder? In a sense, the five books and two stories amounted to a single mega-novel, and it had all been resolved in *Eight Million Ways to Die.* By confronting and owning up to his alcoholism, my protagonist had come to terms with the central problem of his existence. He'd had a catharsis, and what human being, fictional or otherwise, gets more than one of those?

I figured I was done with Scudder. His *d'etre*, you might say, had lost its *raison*. I wished it were otherwise, as I enjoyed seeing the world through his eyes and writing in his voice, but I wasn't willing to force a book into existence.

And that might very well have been the end of it—if not for the third story in this volume, *By the Dawn's Early Light*.

Some years before, Robert J. Randisi told me he was hoping to find a publisher for a collection of original private eye stories. If he managed to do so, would I agree to write a story for the volume? It seemed safe enough to say yes, since the likelihood of my ever hearing further seemed remote at best.

But Bob, the indefatigable founder of Private Eye Writers of America, came to me not long after the publication of *Eight Million Ways to Die* to report success. He'd sold his anthology to Otto Penzler's Mysterious Press, and now he wanted a story from me.

I explained that I seemed to be done with Scudder. Bob was disappointed but understanding. Otto was also understanding, but this didn't stop him from whining and coaxing and wheedling. I explained it was out of the question, and then I went home and figured out how to do it. The story could be a flashback, with a sober Scudder recounting an event from his drinking days.

It worked rather well. Alice Turner snapped it up for *Playboy*, Bob tucked it into his anthology, and MWA gave it an Edgar for Best Short Story. And then a year later I added a couple of additional plot threads to the story and expanded it from 8500 words to 90,000; the resultant novel, *When the Sacred Ginmill Closes*, is the favorite of a good number of Scudder fans.

It was to take several years before I found myself

able to continue the real-time Scudder saga, with his story continuing in his sober years. I picked him up in 1989, with *Out on the Cutting Edge,* and the books have continued to follow at reasonably regular intervals. In 2011, I went back to fill in a gap; *A Drop of the Hard Stuff,* while framed with a late-night conversation between Matt and Mick Ballou, takes place in 1982-3, a year or so after Matt leaves an untouched drink on the bar at the end of *Eight Million Ways to Die.*

And over the years I've continued to write short fiction starring Matthew Scudder. "Batman's Helpers" grew out of a friend's experience in street-level trademark enforcement; Bob Randisi found room for it in *Justice For Hire.* "The Merciful Angel of Death" was written in response to the AIDS crisis, and appeared in *New Mystery,* Jerome Charyn's International Association of Crime Writers anthology.

I've since become friends with Howard Mandel, the jazz authority, but hadn't yet met him when he got in touch through my agent; Howard was promoting a local jazz festival, and thought a short jazz-oriented piece from me, featuring Matt Scudder, might provide a nice highlight for the festival program. "The Night and the Music" was the result, more a vignette than a story, but I liked the way it turned out, and the sense it provided of Matt and Elaine and their particular part of the city. Over the years, it's come to be my performance piece; I tent to trot it out when a short reading is called for.

The next three stories are similar in structure. In each, Scudder looks back on an incident in the past, from his days first as a patrolman and then a detective with the NYPD. In "Looking For David," it's the killer's motive which only comes to light years later, when Matt and Elaine encounter him in Florence. "Let's Get Lost," its title drawn from Chet Baker's haunting song, recalls an ex-officio bit of police work, dating back to when Matt was a married cop and Elaine his hooker girlfriend. And "A Moment of Wrong Thinking" puts the spotlight on Vince Mahaffey, the veteran plainclothes officer with whom Matt was partnered in his early days in Brooklyn. There are references to Mahaffey in several of the novels, but this gives us a closer look at him.

All three of these stories appeared in *Ellery Queen's Mystery Magazine.*

"Mick Ballou Looks at the Blank Screen" was inspired by the final episode of *The Sopranos,* and was written to be the text of a limited-edition broadside produced by Mark Lavendier. Aside from that appearance, it is published here for the first time. Like "The Night and the Music," it's more a vignette than a story, but chronicles an important and perhaps surprising development in Ballou's life. (Though Elaine swears she saw it coming…)

Finally, "One Last Night at Grogan's" brings Matt and Elaine Scudder together with Mick and Kristin Ballou for an evening rich in nostalgia and revelation, one more night with music. The story was written specifically for inclusion in this volume, and has never appeared anywhere before.

LAWRENCE BLOCK

EMAIL: lawbloc@gmail.com
BLOG: http://lawrenceblock.wordpress.com
FACEBOOK: http://www.facebook.com/lawrence.block
WEBSITE: http://www.lawrenceblock.com
TWITTER: @LawrenceBlock